JACOB'S LANDING

DAPHNE GREER

NIMBUS
PUBLISHING
nimbus.ca

Nimbus Publishing Limited
3731 Mackintosh St, Halifax, NS B3K 5A5
(902) 455-4286 nimbus.ca

Printed and bound in Canada

NB1147

Design: Heather Bryan

Library and Archives Canada Cataloguing in Publication

Greer, Daphne, author
Jacob's landing / Daphne Greer.
ISBN 978-1-77108-279-2 (pbk.)

I. Title.
PS8613.R4452J33 2015   jC813'.6   C2014-907763-7

Nimbus Publishing acknowledges the financial support for its publishing activities from the Government of Canada through the Canada Book Fund (CBF) and the Canada Council for the Arts, and from the Province of Nova Scotia through Film & Creative Industries Nova Scotia. We are pleased to work in partnership with Film & Creative Industries Nova Scotia to develop and promote our creative industries for the benefit of all Nova Scotians.

For Mom and Dad, with love.

CHAPTER ONE

I, JACOB MOSHER, AM SENTENCED to two months and a day with Captain Crazy and his sidekick, Pearl.

⤳

"Life throws us pickles, Jacob," Maggie says. "The trick is turning them into something sweet."

Maggie's the closest thing I have to a mum, but she's only my foster one. I never knew my real one. Dad used to say that some mums aren't meant to be mums. I guess I had one of those. Dad said alcohol got the better of her.

Maggie kisses me on the top of my head. "It's only for the summer."

"Maggie's right, Jacob," adds Bernice, my social worker. "This is a miracle, to discover your dad's family."

Just the mention of Dad makes me sad. It's been almost a year since he died, but it feels like yesterday.

Bernice flips through my file. "Jacob, I thought you'd be excited. Don't you want to know your grandparents?"

"What if I don't like them?" I mutter. "Did you ever think about that?" I pick at the hole in my jeans until Maggie squeezes my hand.

"Jacob, we've been over this a hundred times," Bernice carries on. *Blah, blah, blah*. I know she's going to explain for the zillionth time that Maggie is going on some quiet retreat to have a break from everything. I guess she has a few sour pickles herself. I tried talking Bernice out of it—I mean, isn't it illegal to send a kid someplace with really old people he's never met before? It should be.

∽

Two weeks later, after an airplane ride from Ottawa and the longest cab ride ever, I pass a sign that says, *Halfway between the Equator and the North Pole*. I then get dumped off in front of a huge mansion at the top of a hill in the middle of Nova Scotia, a.k.a. nowhere. Next thing I know I'm sitting with Pearl, my grandmother, in a room she keeps calling a parlour—who calls the TV room a parlour? She talks so fast her false teeth keep slipping down. She sucks them up and I can hear her clicking them up to the roof of her mouth.

I've never seen teeth suddenly slip out and stare at you. I can't help watching them.

She keeps looking at me like she's seen a ghost. I stare back at her, partly because she has really black hair and bright red lipstick. I'm starting to wonder if she thinks it's Halloween. You'd think she'd want to ask a few questions about Dad or me. I wonder if she's just as nervous as I am. And then she says, "Well! Let's not waste any more time chit-chatting. Why don't you follow me upstairs? You can tell your grandfather to come down for a cup of tea."

She ushers me out as if she's got something really important to do. I've only been here for five minutes.

The banister creaks and wobbles as she hauls herself up each step as if she weighs three hundred pounds, except she's really scrawny. By the sounds of her huffing and puffing, she needs one of those sit-down stair elevators, the ones that freakishly happy people ride with a basket of laundry on their lap.

"Phew," she says as we reach the second floor. "You'll have to make the rest of the journey on your own. My ticker says I need to sit down for a spell, then I'll make us some tea." Her eyes look worn out when she tells me this.

All of a sudden I feel kind of nauseous. Does that mean she's going to have a heart attack? Maggie said to be helpful and to mind my manners, but I'm no doctor.

"Okay," I say. "But are you sure you're all right?"

"Bless your little heart." She pats me on the shoulder. "I'll be fine. Frank is on the third floor. Don't pay any mind to his bark. It's the old sea captain in him." She then heads towards her bedroom on the right.

She leaves me standing in a hallway the size of four bedrooms put together. You could skateboard up here. I had no idea Dad's parents were loaded! I walk by three of the rooms, trying to figure out which one is mine. There is a pink room, a blue room, and a green room, all neat and tidy and done up to look really old, like time stopped here years ago.

At my room back at Maggie's, I shoved everything under

my bed and in the closet. She's going to be mad when she discovers my dirty laundry mixed in with my clean clothes. Oh, well, I know she's going to miss me, even though she looked kind of relieved to say goodbye to me at the airport.

CLUNK! WHAM! WHOMP!

I peer up the staircase. What is he doing? I'm nervous, but here goes nothing. I cough several times, hoping he'll hear me.

"Batten down the hatches, mates!" a stern voice orders. "There's a storm coming—we need to prepare!"

Who is he talking to?

I listen for a few minutes before knocking on the door.

"Who's there?" he barks.

"It's me, Jacob."

Silence.

I wait a minute. My heart thumps.

"Speak up! Can't hear a thing!" he bellows.

He startles me. My fingers tremble as I place them on the doorknob. "Um…Pearl sent me up," I say through the door. "Can I come in?"

"Of course!" he snaps.

The door creaks open. The old guy is bent over a long telescope, peering into the eyepiece.

"Don't stand there!" he says. "You're needed on deck. Grab the halyards and take in the sails. Didn't you hear my orders? There's a storm coming!" He doesn't even turn to look at me.

"Um…" I clear my throat, hoping maybe he'll start

talking normally any minute. But I figure that's not going to happen: the telescope is pointed right at his bookcase.

"Pearl wants you to come downstairs for tea," I manage to get out.

Franks straightens up and says, "Who did you say you were?"

A loud buzzing blares out of a black box on Frank's bedside table before I can answer.

"That blasted noise!" he growls, making his way to check the box. He grumbles under his breath about some "lazy sod in the galley." He feels his way with his hands, as though his fingers are his eyes.

I think he's blind...weird that Pearl didn't tell me.

"What's the problem?" he yells into the intercom. "Have you put the coal out?"

"Frank Mosher! Stop this nonsense!"

"Who's this?" he demands.

"It's your wife, Frank. It's time to come down for tea. Now snap out of it."

"Bah," he mutters under his breath.

I wonder why Pearl sent me upstairs to get him when she's calling anyway.

"Is Jacob still with you?"

"Who?"

"Your grandson, Frank! I sent him up a few minutes ago."

Frank takes off his sailor's cap and scratches his head.

"The boy? Yes—yes, he's accounted for."

"Jacob, dear, are you all right?"

"Yeah, I'm fine."

"Well hurry down, you two, the tea is laid out."

Frank plunks down on his bed. The medals on his jacket clink together. He reaches into his checkered pants and pulls out a white handkerchief to wipe the sweat off his forehead.

"Right then, let's go to the galley for tea."

CHAPTER TWO

FRANK GRABS A WHITE CANE by his bedside table and stands up. He starts swinging it back and forth in front of him.

"Well don't just stand there. Open the door, boy."

How does he know what I'm doing? I scramble towards the door and hold it open, moving out of Frank's way so he doesn't bash me in the shins with his cane. He holds on to the banister with his right hand. His feet seem to glide down the stairs on autopilot. He doesn't start using his cane again until he's on the last step. Halfway down the hallway, he stops. "How old are you, sailor?"

"Twelve."

"And what part of the country have you come from?"

"Ottawa."

"A little young to be out on the high seas, aren't you? Trouble on the home front?"

Before I have time to answer, he says, "Do you know how many steps it takes to get down to the galley from the bridge?"

"Um…no."

"I'll expect an answer at briefing time."

He starts walking. Just like that.

When we reach the main floor, my suitcase is still sitting where I left it—next to the front door, which is wide open. I guess out here in the boonies they don't worry about break-ins.

The twang of country music plays on the TV. I follow Frank into the big kitchen. The table is cluttered with papers and trays of leftover food. Pill bottles are scattered on the counter. Right in the middle of the room is a staircase wide enough for five people to stand side by side. At the top of the stairs the door is closed. I feel like running up and down them for fun. I mean, who has a staircase in the middle of their kitchen? Where does it go?

Frank walks to the back of the house and out to the sun porch. The sound of a tractor in the back field rumbles close to the house.

"I wish Harold would stop cutting the hay long enough for us to think," Pearl says looking outside. "He's had that thing going since seven this morning."

Soon the tractor sounds are gone and it's quiet...too quiet. Rolling hills sink down to meet the water. There are no cars zooming past, no horns blowing, no loud music from someone else's apartment. I'm going to go crazy.

"Sugar and milk?" Pearl asks as she pours tea into little fancy teacups.

"Yeah, sure," I say, as if I have it all the time. Maggie's a big health nut and doesn't let me have any caffeine.

Dad liked tea.

Pearl stares at me again. "It's really great that Maggie offered you up for the summer. The girl who used to come in to help me with the cooking and cleaning every day just up and left two days ago."

I drop my teacup. It rattles on the saucer and tea sloshes out. I'm the new help? I remember Maggie and Bernice saying something about *helping out,* but nothing about *being the helper.* Isn't this supposed to be reunion time? Sort of a makeup for the years they didn't even know they had a grandson? Picnics, looking at old photos, going to the beach—that kind of thing?

"I actually like having my place back to myself." Pearl carries on as if I asked her a question, which I clearly didn't. "The girl was always poking into my business, you know, and telling me how to do things. I know perfectly well how things need to be done." She takes a big slurp of tea. "We still have people coming in to help Frank every morning with, you know, things of a personal nature. So you don't have to worry about that."

That's a relief.

She leans in towards me, as if she's going to tell me a big secret. I can hardly wait.

"Frank started mixing up shaving cream with toothpaste and not wanting to clean his privates." Her eyes get wide.

It's weird how she talks about him as if he isn't here. I look over at him. He's sitting quietly in a big chair. Actually, I think he's asleep.

"There'll be lots of things you can help me with," Pearl says, pouring more tea for herself. "Now, I must tell you, a young lad named Wendell comes in to help me with errands. He's the salt of the earth." She goes on and on about Wendell, and then stops suddenly. "We'll get along fine. I can just tell." She pats my knee and gives me a big smile. Luckily, her teeth stay in place.

I force a smile, but inside I'm rehearsing what I'm going to say to Maggie over the phone.

CHAPTER THREE

"COME OVER HERE, DEAR. I won't bite," Pearl says, patting the piano bench later on that afternoon. Her feet barely touch the floor. A music stand and two uncomfortable-looking sofas are in the front room, while a fake poodle stands guard at the door. Having no polite way to decline, I join her.

Before I can sit down, Pearl is belting out church hymns like it's a normal thing to do. It's not even Sunday.

"*I can't hear you*," she sings. Her voice raises a couple of octaves to get her point across.

She can't be serious. The more she sings, the harder it is to stop myself from smirking. I turn my head, then look back at the music. I make an attempt to join in on "Onward Christian Soldiers," but my voice just cracks and quivers.

"You're not much of a singer, are you?" she says at the end of the hymn. "I'm a little disappointed that duets might not be in the picture for the two of us."

"I guess it's not really my thing." The piano bench creaks as I shift in my seat. There's an awkward silence.

"Well, your father loved to sing!"

"He did?"

"Well of course he did. He also had the best timing. He never missed a beat."

Pearl rummages through some sheet music and pulls out a worn piece called "Spirit of Life."

"This was his favourite." Her knobby fingers navigate the keys as if by heart. The wrinkles on her forehead seem to vanish while she's singing. The song is vaguely familiar.

All of a sudden, I find myself thinking about stuff—stuff that's hidden. Pearl is right. Dad was good with time, right down to the last second.

Except on the day he never showed.

I bite my lip, to push that stuff away again.

"I would have played it myself at his funeral, had I known. I don't think I'll ever get over missing it."

Her words hang in the air like a thick black cloud. I don't really know what to say.

Two months? No way. I'm not going to last.

I haul my suitcase onto the bed and start rummaging through it. I know it's here somewhere—it just has to be. Finally, after dumping everything out, I remember the zipper on the side pocket. Sure enough, it's there.

Phew.

I am so relieved to see his face. Dad *loved* to sing? I wonder what makes a person stop doing things they love. It's weird that there aren't any pictures of him around here. They're his parents, so you'd think they'd have at least one—even Maggie has a couple of pictures of me in the living room.

I phone Maggie. The answering machine kicks in. I slam the receiver down and then dial again, just in case she's screening her calls. She started doing that after Jim left.

"Maggie! Pick up! It's me, Jacob." I hang up and stare at the phone, waiting for her to ring back.

She doesn't.

Then I remember she's probably left for her retreat. Sighing, I walk over to the window and push it up as far as it will go. The night air smells different here. The moon is full and the sky is jam-packed with a zillion stars. Light flickers on the water.

Back at Maggie's, the sky would be lit up from street lights and people's apartments and offices. I miss her already.

Pearl and Frank have gone to bed. I'm sleeping in the pink room. Not sure why. You'd think, seeing as I'm a guy, they'd have given me the blue room.

I flop down onto the bed and pick up the phone again. This time I dial Bernice, but I hang up when I hear her voice on the answering machine. I don't even know why I called her. She'd just do her counselling thing, where she repeats back everything I say to her. It drives me nuts.

I lie there for a few minutes staring at Dad's picture, trying to see if he looks like Frank or Pearl. But I can't see either of them in him.

Dad, why didn't you tell me about them?

It's a long story… I can hear him say. It was his standard answer when I'd ask him what Mum was like, until the day I hit a sore spot and he said, "Look! Your mum chose alcohol over you! The court papers even said so." I don't think he meant to be so mean, maybe he just didn't know what else to say. Maggie says some people are good talkers and some aren't. I learned to stop asking. That was when it became easier to think of Mum as being dead.

A train whistle blows off in the distance, snapping me back. I tuck Dad's picture underneath my pillow.

I'm wide awake.

I'll never get to sleep. I try to get comfortable and then find myself rolling over in my bed to see how many times I can make it before falling out. One—two—three—four rolls. It's way bigger than my single bed at Maggie's.

I lie there, trying to get used to all the different noises. Outside, a high-pitched peeping sound drifts through the window, and off in the distance a dog is barking. Then I hear a growling noise that goes up and down, like the house is haunted or something. Maybe that's why Dad never came back.

The growling sound gets louder. I slip out of bed and open my bedroom door to see where it's coming from. Moonlight spills into the hallway. I tiptoe towards the sound, trying not to let the floorboards squeak. It's definitely coming from Pearl's room.

Oh, great. She snores.

I close the door and flop back onto my bed. The headboard crashes into the wall, making a loud bang. "Oh, man!" I dive under the covers and the headboard bangs louder.

Then there's a knock on my door. I feel my heart race as I come up for air. Pearl stands in my doorway wearing a long nightie that goes right to the floor. She waves a flashlight around. "Ah yoo all whide, acob? I dus heah a wow bang." Her words sound strange, sort of like when I stuff my mouth with marshmallows and try to talk, and she kind of looks like one of those dried-up apple dolls people sell at the market.

Oh, I get it. She doesn't have her teeth in.

"Yeah, I'm okay. I kind of banged the headboard by mistake."

"Oh, da's a welief. I didn' mow ip ih was wank walling oud ob bed."

The next morning I wake to the annoying sound of Pearl's doorbell.

Ding-dong. Ding-dong. DING-DONG.

What time is it? The sun streams into my room, making the pink walls look like bubblegum.

DING-DONG. DING-DONG.

"Okay, okay…I'm coming." I whip off the blankets and pad over to the window. A green car is parked out front. I make my way down the stairs, taking the last two in one leap.

Standing on the front step is a short, fat lady with sunken, flabby cheeks. Her eyes are small and dark. "What took you so long? I've been standing out here for fifteen minutes!" She talks to me like we've met a hundred times as she brushes past me to hang up her sweater.

I glance at the clock in the front hall. It's only seven o'clock. Who rings doorbells this early?

"I don't suppose he's up yet," she says, glancing up the staircase.

Then I put two and two together: she must be Frank's morning help.

"Uh…I don't think so. It's kind of quiet around here."

"Well, I have a list of people as long as my arm to tend to," she complains as she climbs the stairs. Then she stops and turns around. "You must be the grandson Pearl has been going on about."

"Yeah, that's me."

"Some folks around here say it's a bit strange it's taken you so long to come for a visit, but that's none of my business." She then heads up the stairs.

That kinda stings, but I reluctantly follow her. I'm not sure I'd want her waking me up in the morning. What a crabby lady!

Pearl appears from her room just as we reach the landing at the first floor. She's wearing a hairnet. "Oh, dood. Yoaw heah!"

Oh God. Her teeth still aren't in. She looks like she's about to swallow her cheeks.

"Of course I'm here, Pearl. I've been outside for the past fifteen minutes!"

Wow! She's even crabby to Pearl. I watch her waddle down the hall and up the flight of stairs to see Frank.

Pearl pulls me into her room, shuts the door, puts her fingers to her mouth, and says, "Shhhhh." She pokes her head back out into the hallway. "I don' dwust *dat* one," she whispers, closing the bedroom door behind her.

I'm not sure what's going on. Pearl pokes her head out the door one more time. Her bedroom is bigger than Maggie's kitchen and living room put together. A huge wooden four-poster bed with lots of carving on it barely takes up any space.

Pearl shuts the door. Her eyes have a determined look. She goes to say something, but then stops herself. She points her finger at me as if to say, "Just a minute," then walks over to her bedside table, where her teeth sit at the bottom of a cup of water. I try not to stare at them, but can't help myself. I picture them screaming to get out.

She pulls them out of the cup. Droplets of water drip onto the floor. She gives her teeth a little wipe with her nightie, and then shoves them into her mouth.

Gross.

She clicks them to the roof of her mouth a few times then whispers, "*That one* keeps talking about how Frank should be in a nursing home, as if *she* knows what's good for him."

She grabs me by the shoulders. I feel her fingers dig in a little. "You'll keep an eagle eye on her, won't you? Frank may cause me grief at times, but I'm still his wife, and I'll be darned if some nosy, no-good helper is going to tell me what I should do!"

Pearl's eyes soften as she pats my shoulder. "You're a good boy, Jacob. I can tell." She takes off her hairnet and glances at herself in the mirror. "Oh, my—I'm a bit much in the morning, aren't I?" She plunks herself down at the foot of the bed and sighs. "They used to call me Pearly Toes at dances, you know." She holds onto the post and stretches out her legs, whose purple and red bulging veins look like they're going to pop any minute and squirt blood everywhere. She immediately covers them up with her nightie. "I don't suppose you like to dance?"

"Not really."

"Well, that's too bad, dear. There's nothing like a good dance partner."

CHAPTER FOUR

"YEEHAW!" I HEAR FROM OUTSIDE.

I run to the back sun porch to see what's going on, but all I see is a red bike flying down the lane.

Man, people get up early here.

"Ahem!"

Startled, I turn around. The Crab is wedged in the doorway, holding an empty toilet paper bag. "Tell Pearl she needs more."

"Uh, yeah, okay."

"Frank will be downstairs in a while. He's talking foolish again, telling me to pull in the sails. It's a load of crap, if you ask me." She shakes her head. "They don't pay me enough to put up with this."

I can't believe she's telling me this. She must hate her job. When I'm older I'm going to make sure I love mine.

She hands me the empty bag. "Make sure Pearl gets the right kind. He says this is like sandpaper." The Crab waddles back through the kitchen and into the front hallway, grabs her sweater, and slips out the front door without saying goodbye.

I plunk down on the staircase, resting my head in my

hands. The wall clock ticks each second. My stomach grumbles. It's going to take forever to get to the end of the summer.

BUZZZZZZZZZZZZZZZZZZZZZZZZZZZZZZ!

I bolt off the stairs and search for Frank's buzzer. He must be slamming the button a zillion times.

BUZZZZZZZZZZZZZ! BUZZZZZZZZZZZZZ! BUZZZZZZZZZZZZZZZZZZZZZZZZZ!

The machine on the hall table flashes a red light, and I push the only button there is. "Hello?"

"Who's this?" Frank bellows.

"Me—Jacob."

"Who?"

"Jacob...remember?"

Frank pauses. I can hear him breathing into the intercom.

"Oh, the boy. Right. Yes. Well, is she gone?"

"Who?" Now I'm sounding like Frank.

"The morning warrant officer."

He must mean The Crab. "Yup," I grin. "She just left."

"Good. I'll be right down." The flashing light stops.

This place feels nuttier by the minute. I wish Pearl would hurry up and get out of the tub. At least she's used to Frank.

I pace back and forth in the front hallway, willing Pearl to arrive before him. Instead, I hear Frank's cane clicking away on the floors above me as he makes his way down.

"What's the weather like outside?" he asks from the top steps. He carries binoculars around his neck and wears the same suit jacket he had on yesterday, full of his medals that clink and clank as he heads down the stairs.

"Looks okay, I guess…I haven't really been outside yet."

"Well, stick your nose outside, boy. I need an accurate report."

Outside, the smell of the rose bushes hangs in the air. I hear Maggie's voice in my head: *It's a picture-perfect day.*

"I think it's going to be a nice day," I tell him.

"Think or know?"

"Know," I say, standing up straighter.

"Good answer. Now, what's the time of day?"

I glance at the hall clock. "Seven-fifty," I say, this time with some *knowing* in my voice.

"Well, don't just stand there, sailor. We've only have a few minutes to raise the flag."

He heads straight to the coat rack, feeling for a duffle bag hanging from the top rung.

"Grab this and follow me. We've got morning colours to attend to." His cane flickers back and forth in front of him until he finds the front door.

"Are you sure it's—"

Frank completely ignores me, striding out the door and down the front steps with his slippers still on. He steps off the path and crosses the lawn. "Now, where is that blasted post?" he mumbles.

"You're headed towards the ditch!" I dump the duffle bag and scramble towards him, guiding him back up to the safety of the lawn. "Are you, um, looking for the flagpole, Frank?"

"Of course I am. And during morning colours, it's Captain to you."

"Um…okay, Captain. It's this way."

He holds my elbow and lets me lead the way.

"We're at the flagpole."

"Good navigating, boy."

He was never more than a few feet away from it, but he makes it sound like we've just manoeuvred a ship on the high seas.

"Do you have the flag ready?"

"Oh, I'll go get it." I zip back to where I left it in the grass.

"Have you ever raised a flag, boy?"

"Um…no."

Frank mumbles something under his breath, stepping closer to the pole until he touches it. Then he feels his way down to the base of it.

"Hi, Captain."

I whirl around. A girl jumps off a red bike. She has jet-black hair and huge blue eyes. She takes off her helmet and throws it on the ground. "Sorry I'm late."

"Late? You haven't been here for days!" Frank growls.

"I know. I've been away at camp. Do you want some help?" she asks.

"Of course I want help. And while you're at it, show the boy the drill."

"Hi, I'm Ruby. Who are you?"

"Jacob."

"We don't have time for small talk," Frank says. "Time is ticking!"

"Sorry, Captain," Ruby says. "So, have you ever tied a reef knot?" she asks me.

I shrug my shoulders. "Maybe—I mean, I probably have, and just haven't *called* it a reef knot."

"Show me, then." She hands me the rope.

Why did I have to say that?

I make my way to the flagpole. How hard can it be? I fumble with the rope and tie it the only way I know how.

"Nice try," Ruby says, smiling. "Might as well learn it straight up, the way The Captain showed me." She bends down and grabs the rope and starts tying the knot. "Right over left and under, then left over right and under. Got it? And then we just slip this through here, so it makes it easier to raise."

"We don't call it a reef knot where I'm from," I say under my breath.

"What's the time, Coxswain?" The Captain asks.

"Seven fifty-nine," Ruby answers. "One minute to morning colours, Captain."

"Right, then." Frank reaches into his pocket and pulls out a long silver object that curves into a little ball at the end. He holds it out for Ruby. She studies her watch, and at exactly eight o'clock she puts the object to her mouth and blows one long, loud whistle. It makes a high-pitched, piercing sound. I plug my ears. Several crows scatter from a nearby tree.

The Captain stands straight as a board, his right hand rigid in a salute position just under his bushy eyebrows. Ruby finally stops blowing the whistle.

"Do you want to raise it?" she asks me.

I shake my head. I'm not messing up twice.

"Suit yourself." Ruby raises the Canadian flag. There's no wind, so it hangs limp at the top. She scurries over to the side of the house, where a big bell sits on a cement pedestal. She clangs it twice, waits a second, clangs it twice again, waits, then repeats the pattern several more times. The sound vibrates in my chest.

Frank's hand shakes as he holds his position. I look around to see if anyone is watching us. I'm starting to think Frank is running a secret boot camp here for all the local kids.

On the sixth clang of the bell, Pearl's voice rings out: "Frank Mosher!"

She's leaning out the upper window. Ruby keeps striking the bell and Frank stares straight ahead as if he can't hear her.

"I've been looking all over for you, Frank!" she yells.

After the eighth set of rings, Ruby squints up to Pearl. "Mornin', Pearl," she says. "Sorry, I couldn't stop until the last bell was rung. You know the drill."

"Yes, Ruby. I know *the drill*. Eight rings of the bell to let the whole community of Newport Landing know it's eight bloody o'clock! I take it you're back from camp, are you?"

"Yup. Got in last night."

"So I guess we're back to this nonsense, are we Frank?!" She slams the window shut.

Ruby's eyes go wide. "Well, guess I better go. I'll be back at sunset, Captain. I'll see you around, Jacob."

CHAPTER FIVE

"I WANT TO KNOW WHEN you're going out to that darn flagpole," Pearl says, leaning over a pot of boiling water. She's all pinked out, wearing a pink housecoat and pink knitted slippers to match.

Frank shuffles through the kitchen and doesn't answer her.

"Did you hear me, Frank?"

"Hard not to," he says under his breath.

Pearl grabs me as I'm walking by. "I'm glad you're here, Jacob. I've had to rescue that stubborn mule from the ditch too many times. He gets me so riled up!"

I'm not sure what to say. Before I have time to answer, she pours coffee into two cups, adds a splosh of milk in one, plops a bunch of sugar cubes in both, and stirs them.

She places them on a tray and acts as if nothing were upsetting her. "Frank's in the dining room—hurry along, dear. He likes his coffee hot." She hands me the tray and then ushers me out of the kitchen. I guess old people just like to tell you stuff.

The dining room is surrounded by windows overlooking the water. A huge table sits in the middle, with porcelain girls holding flowers placed all over it. But it's the old paintings hanging on the walls that kind of freak me out. The people in them don't look so happy. None of them are smiling. Everyone is dressed in black except for a little boy dressed in a sailor suit. The man is sitting on a chair and the woman has her hand resting on his shoulder. You'd think in a family portrait they'd at least look like they're enjoying themselves. Instead, they stare right at me as if they're watching my every move. No wonder Dad never wanted to come here. The place is really sketchy.

Frank sits crammed in the corner of the room at a smaller round table.

"Here's your coffee," I say.

He taps the top of the table until his fingertips find the cup.

"Good. It's piping hot. Just the way I like it. You've done well, boy."

"Well, actually…Pearl made it."

"Oh, crab fish." He slides his cup closer to himself and sniffs it. "Is the milk curdling, boy?"

"Um…curdling?"

"Do you see anything floating in my coffee?"

I lean over his cup. "It looks normal to me."

Pearl comes into the room holding a tray. "Get your nose out of the coffee, Frank. The milk is fine!" The tray wobbles and the dishes clink together. She places it down with a heavy sigh. I reach over to catch the egg cups before they topple over.

"Thank you, dear. I hope you like soft-boiled eggs. There's always so much racket in the news about eating too many eggs. But Frank and I have survived just fine—haven't we, Frank?"

"What is the tide doing, boy?"

"I think it's coming in," I say, glancing out the window.

"You mean flooding, boy. You sound like a landlubber!"

Pearl sits down with a thump. "He never answers me. It's like I'm invisible." She makes a face at Frank.

"The old *Rotundus* will be making her way down to the landing once it's high water," Frank announces. "Pearl, you should send the boy into Windsor to get some more milk."

"Frank! The *Rotundus* hasn't come this way for eighty–four years. Honestly," she says, shaking her head. "Besides, the milk is fine."

Frank digs into his egg cup like he's in a race.

We sit for the longest time in awkward silence. Frank chomps away at his toast while Pearl sighs and stares at the flooding tide coming in.

Fifty-six more breakfasts.

"What's the *Rotundus*?" I finally ask to break the silence.

"Oh, Jacob." Pearl pats my knee. "It was a ship. Well, actually it was a steam-powered ferry boat." Her eyes light up and she starts talking quickly. "It was such a grand thing. People would be all dressed up in their fancy hats to go into Windsor. Now people don't give a darn about their appearance. The other day I saw a lady with curlers in her hair at the grocery store! I think it's downright disgraceful."

I shouldn't have asked.

Pearl goes on and on about the ferry boat and this person and that person. "I only wish that I could have sailed on it. I was born the year it stopped sailing in Newport Landing. But it's our little treasure and I'll boast about it until the day I die. A shame it sank years later."

"The boy just needs fifty cents for a round trip," Frank mumbles.

"That's right, Frank—it *used* to cost fifty cents when you were a little boy. He's much older than me," Pearl whispers.

I'm now caught in a tug-of-war between Captain Crazy and Pearl.

"People would have about two hours to get their shopping done before the tide started going back out."

Maggie says it's good to be silent, so you can be still with your thoughts. "Stop talking!" my thoughts are screaming. Somehow, I don't think that's what Maggie means.

"It cruises at ten knots, boy, and always returns on the same tide. Do you know how fast ten knots is?" Frank asks.

"No," I mumble. I'm hoping if I don't show any interest, they might get the hint. Besides, it's not as if we learn all this in school. But I don't dare say that to him. He'd have me doing push-ups if I told him that.

"I'll expect an answer at briefing time." Frank takes a big slurp of his coffee and leans back in his chair.

Pearl's face lights up. "Frank, remember your father telling us about the *Rotundus* and its midnight excursions when the band went along?"

"Can't say I do."

"Well, I remember it as plain as day. Having to listen to him at great lengths over a glass of sherry." Pearl pushes herself up from the table and walks over to the stereo in the corner. "Your parents went on their first date on the *Rotundus*. Remember, Frank?" She opens up the cover, lifts an arm thing, and carefully places it on a record.

"This might jog your memory. Your father played this song every time he told us the story."

Crackle and more crackle blares out of a speaker before a jolt of trumpets and clarinets explodes into a crazy musical concert.

A smile tugs at the corner of Frank's mouth.

"Come dance with me," Pearl says, and then tries to get Frank to stand up. His smile quickly fades and a look of irritation takes over.

"Stop your foolishness, Pearl! I'm not dancing. Can't you see I'm trying to eat my breakfast?"

"Oh, humbug yourself!" Pearl says and then storms out of the room.

Thanks to Pearl, I'm now stuck sitting with Frank, listening to their ancient music. I keep hoping he's going to get up and turn it off—but no such luck.

Every now and then I glance over at him. He looks like he's deep in thought. Maybe he *is* remembering.

CHAPTER SIX

"THERE YOU ARE," PEARL SAYS, joining me out on the front porch. "You're just like your dad. He used to sit out here and watch the world go by."

What world? I haven't even seen a car yet.

Pearl is dressed for town. She's wearing a bright green dress and clutching a green purse with flowers on it.

Wow.

Her eyebrows, absent at breakfast, now match her black hair. I still can't believe she's seventy-eight years old. Shouldn't her hair be grey? I'm starting to think she lied to Bernice and Maggie about her age, 'cause she sure didn't tell them about her help quitting on her.

Pearl looks at her watch. "Wendell should be here any minute."

Sure enough, two seconds later a truck with a loud muffler zooms over the hill. The driver honks the horn, turns into the lane, and then backs up so that he's parked right in front of the house.

"Do you want to come with us? We're going to do some errands. I could show you around Windsor."

"Um…I'm actually kind of tired. Is it okay if I just stay here?"

Pearl's face drops, but I still can't bring myself to go.

Wendell gets out of the truck. He's tall and skinny with a ball cap on his head and an unlit cigar tucked into the corner of his mouth. "Mornin', Pearl." He holds the door open for her. "You must be Jacob. It's good to see some family finally out here. You're all Pearl's been talking about."

I feel kind of bad when I hear that. I wish I knew why Dad wrote them off.

Wendell helps Pearl into the front seat of the truck. "What will Frank do while you're gone?" I ask her.

"Oh, don't you worry about him. He'll be fine. He'll probably sleep away most of the morning. You can go exploring if you'd like." She glances at herself in the side-view mirror and adjusts her hair. "If you want to be an angel, though, you could do the dishes. I might have left a few."

"You're starting to miss all your lady help, aren't you, Pearl?" Wendell chuckles. "I reckon you've got to go easier on the next batch they send you."

"Don't you start in on me, Wendell. You're not so perfect yourself. It's not too much trouble is it, Jacob?" Her eyes plead with me.

"Yeah, I'll do them."

She sticks her arm out and squeezes my hand. "Thank you, dear."

Wendell starts his truck up. The muffler roars like thunder as they go up and over the hill. Pearl's little hand waves out the window.

DAPHNE GREER

I decide to walk down the lane. The dishes can wait.

There's a sweet smell in the air, like a perfume department. I think it's coming from the huge trees lining the property.

Halfway down is a big barn. To the left is an apple orchard, and to the right there's a car garage. The windows are pretty dirty. I rub one of the panes with my sleeve and peek in.

A voice shouts, "That's a 1951 Cadillac."

I whirl around. Ruby jumps down from one of the trees. "That's The Captain's. He used to drive it all over the place until his eyesight went. It's pretty neat, eh?"

"What are you doing out here?" I'm not sure I like the way she appears out of nowhere.

"Oh, I always come out here. My house is too crazy. Besides, I was waiting to see how long you'd last. I figured you'd get pretty bored with Pearl and The Captain. Do you want me to show you around?"

"Uh, no thanks. I'm okay."

"Oh, come on. You got something better to do?"

She has a point. "Yeah, all right."

"Good! I'll get you a bike. That way we can cover more ground. Be right back."

Ruby runs up the lane and over to her house. She comes back a few minutes later with a black bike. "This should fit you."

"Thanks."

She walks over to the tree and grabs her bike. "I'll

34

take you to Rock Cove and then to the graveyard. Come on."

I follow Ruby down the lane. It's full of potholes and puddles. She zigzags around as if she knows them by heart. When we get to the top of the hill, she lets go of her handlebars and coasts out into the field with her feet sticking way out.

I realize I'm grinning from ear to ear when I feel the wind brushing against my face and my mouth starts going dry.

"There's Rock Cove!" Ruby says pointing towards the water.

I look over the cliff and see where a bunch of boulders meet the water's edge.

"Come on! We've got to beat the tide." Ruby flies down the hill.

Pearl and Frank's house is way off in the distance. From here it looks like it's standing guard for the community; the houses next to it look so small.

"Come on! The tide will cover the mud soon!"

I coast down the hill with my brakes squeaking all the way. Ruby waits for me at the bottom, before scrambling over rocks and boulders. She plunks herself down on a rock that sort of looks like a chair. "Isn't this cool? I even have a footrest." She gets comfortable stretching out. "You can sit in that one." She points to another rock.

The water looks like chocolate milk. I like the sound it makes as it laps against the rocks.

"I bet you don't have anything like this where you live."

I'm suddenly reminded of back home. It seems so far away now. I'm even having trouble picturing it. "Nah, nothing like this." I glance over where I just saw rocks. They're almost covered with water. "The tide comes in pretty fast."

Ruby glances at her watch. "Yeah, we've probably got another ten minutes before we're goners." She laughs. "Nah, you're right. We should probably motor."

Her words hit me square in the chest. That was Dad's saying. *Come on, Jacob—we should motor.* Suddenly, I find myself really missing him.

"You all right?"

"Yeah, I was just thinking about…it's nothing. Hey, what's over there?" I point across the water, trying to take my mind off him.

"That's Windsor to the left—straight ahead is Falmouth, and further down to the right is Hantsport. When the tide is completely out, you can walk across the mud to the other side. We go mud sliding there. I'll take you sometime if you want."

"Mud sliding?" I look at her like she's nuts.

"It's the best ever. You run and dive smack into the mud and slide down until you hit the water."

I can just hear my friends back home when I tell them I've gone mud sliding! They won't believe me.

"We'd better get out of here." Ruby stands up and heads away from the water.

There's nothing but blue sky and wide open fields awaiting us. There's a creek separating the lower fields from each other. The grass is up to our knees. My wheels collect bits of it that make a funny ticking sound every time I pedal.

"This is Clover Field," Ruby yells back at me. "Can you smell the clover?"

I think she must name every place she steps foot on. By the time we reach the graveyard, which sits on a hill, I'm gasping for air.

"You don't do much, do you?" Ruby says. "What do you do for fun where you live? Obviously you don't bike, or run, or move around at all."

"I don't know. Stuff. You know…"

I sit down in the grass to catch my breath and think for a minute. I feel kind of stupid that I don't have a better answer, but Dad loved the outdoors, and after he died I kind of stopped doing fun things that reminded me of him.

Maggie tries to get me out doing stuff, but I usually find an excuse not to. It has really been getting under her skin.

"So?"

"I'm thinking." I grab bunches of grass and pitch them in front of me.

"How come you haven't visited Pearl and The Captain before?"

Her question catches me off guard. "I don't know." It seems like another dumb answer, but I really don't have a clue. "My dad never mentioned them."

"Why don't you ask him?"

My stomach tightens.

"I can't. He's dead."

"Oh, geez. I'm sorry." Ruby says. "I didn't know."

She's quiet for a few moments before she asks, "How about your mum? Would she know?"

I pitch the handful of grass I've been tearing. "She's dead too."

I don't bother telling Ruby that I have no sweet clue where my mum is or what she even looks like.

CHAPTER SEVEN

"I'm really sorry," Ruby says.

"It's okay. It's not your fault."

Ruby picks up a scraggy red bouquet of plastic flowers lying in the grass.

"Those look pretty bad," I say.

"Not to me," Ruby says. She then heads towards a small headstone sitting all by itself at the far end of the graveyard.

I start thinking about all the dead bodies under my feet. Dad was cremated, so at least I know his body isn't full of bugs right now.

I get up. The soft gravel on the path that weaves in and around the graves crunches underneath my feet. By staying on the path I avoid stepping on the gravesites. They don't seem to bother Ruby as she walks around. I wish I were more like that.

"I always feel sorry for this one. She's all alone way over here," Ruby says, placing the bouquet next to the farthest gravestone. "You have family buried here. Do you want to see?"

"Um…I'm not sure." It's still kind of weird to think

I've had family this whole time.

"Come on! You gotta see this gravesite." Ruby leads me to the centre of the graveyard.

A huge gravestone about six feet high with a ship's anchor carved on the top sits on the hill:

CAPTAIN FRANK MOSHER 1824–1909.

"I bet The Captain was named after him," Ruby says. She points out a bunch of other headstones. "Check out their names!"

I can't believe it. All three wives were named Pearl. "Weird!"

"This one has me stumped, though." She bends down to a small, square, granite plaque lying flat in the grass. It's next to one of the Mosher headstones. It's cracked and missing some words. Ruby pulls the grass away from it. On the plaque it reads:

J. J. DEARLY LOVED BY ALL 1961–1969.

"They weren't very old," Ruby says. "Kinda weird they don't have the person's full name, hey?"

"Maybe it was a pet."

"I never thought of that," Ruby says, standing up.

All of a sudden, a dog comes barrelling towards us, and practically knocks Ruby over.

"Poppy! What are you doing here?"

The dog licks her face and then starts jumping up on me.

"She's forever taking off. Poppy! Get down!" Ruby grabs her by the collar. "I better take her home. If we start riding she'll follow us. Come on, Poppy! Let's go, girl!" Ruby leads the way through the orchard. Poppy is sniffing at the grass and chasing anything that moves.

When we get up to Pearl's house, Ruby says, "I guess I'll see you at sunset?"

"Sunset?"

"Yeah, that's when The Captain lowers the flag. You'll get used to the routine. How long are you here for?"

"The whole summer." My shoulders slump.

"That's great! You might as well keep the bike. You'll get plenty of use out of it. See ya tonight."

When I discover something great about being here all summer, I'll let her know.

~

"I can't believe I'm doing this!" I mutter out loud. I gather up the dishes and dump them into the sink.

There's more than a few of them.

"I better not be doing dishes all freaking summer."

Once I'm finished washing, I stick my head around the corner to see if Frank is still in the dining room. Sure enough, he's fast asleep in his chair. I back away quietly. The last thing I want is another quiz about life on the sea—and with Pearl gone I have no one to save me.

I decide to see where the stairs in the kitchen go. Maggie

would think they were the coolest thing. I climb up.

The door at the top of the stairs opens into a narrow hallway. There's a door on the left. I try opening it, but it's locked. Opposite, there's another door. I turn the handle, half expecting it to be locked too. Instead, it opens into a closet. It smells musty, as if no one has been in here for a long time.

A built-in wooden ladder goes up a narrow opening. I step on the first rung and peer up. There's a faint stream of sunshine from a small, round skylight way up. The ladder looks safe enough, so I decide to climb up. At the top there's a hatch. It takes all my strength to push it open.

The warm summer air hits me as I climb out onto a small deck.

Oh, man. This is wild!

I'm on the roof of the house. This is crazy cool. I can see everything. I lean over the railing. Whoa! It's a long way down. There's just enough room to take about five steps left or right. A small telescope is mounted on top of the iron railing.

Man, they really have a thing for telescopes.

I whirl it around, checking out the water, the orchard, all the farmhouses, the road, and then Ruby's house.

Hey, what's that? I focus the eyepiece to get a better look. There's a girl walking on the roof. She lays a blanket down, puts her long, blond hair into a ponytail, and starts reading a magazine.

Who is she?

A dog starts barking and she looks in its direction. I jar the telescope towards the road and then across the water to Windsor.

The girl is lying on her back when I look over again. A car pulls into her driveway. All of a sudden she sits up and glances over in my direction.

I fall to the floor and lie there for a few minutes. I hope she didn't see me. I'll die if she did. I crawl to the opening and close the hatch behind me.

I try to act as though I've just been hanging out in the kitchen when Pearl arrives home a little while later. "Dishes are all done," I say proudly.

"That's lovely, dear. Could you go and help Wendell now?"

"Yeah, sure."

Wendell hands me an armful of bags and then says, "Was that you up on the widow's walk? I bet you've never seen anything like that in Ottawa."

"Nope." I feel my face getting red.

By the time I return with more groceries, Pearl is sitting at the kitchen table. Wendell brings in the last set of bags and dumps them on the floor. "Well, I think I'll be on my way."

"That's fine, Wendell." Pearl rubs her neck. "That plum took the energy right out of me. I'll ring you later." She places her hand over her chest. "I must lie down for a spell. But before I do that, I'd fancy a nice cup of tea. Be an angel, Jacob, and put the kettle on for me. And while we're waiting for that to boil, if it's not too much trouble, could you put the groceries away? You're such a strong lad, it shouldn't take but a minute."

I don't really have a choice, so I say, "Yeah, sure."

Pearl points me toward the various cupboards as if she's a traffic cop directing cars. It's when I get to the freezer that I'm totally stumped. In order to put anything in, I have to pull out a big plastic bag of what looks like...*bed sheets?*

"Um, what's *this* doing in here?"

"Oh, that's where they've been! I've been looking for those sheets. The day little miss Julie up and left me, she was supposed to do the ironing. I didn't have the energy, so I put the sheets in the freezer. Once an iron takes to those, they'll be fit for the Queen of England. There is nothing worse than wrinkled bed sheets. Don't you find?"

"Um...yeah, sort of." I think she's losing her marbles. Good thing she can't see the crumpled heap of sheets I left at the bottom of my bed. "So what do you want me to do with them?"

"Well, if we need the room in the freezer, it looks like today's going to be ironing day. I don't suppose you could run an iron over them while I take a lie-down?"

I'm not sure if this is the time to tell her I've never ironed before.

"I love ironing, myself, but just don't have it in me

these days. You know, I was quite a spunky gal once. They called me Whirly Pearly. I could whip through this house in no time."

She takes a deep breath just as the kettle starts whistling, then gives me instructions on how to make the tea just right. "No sense in spoiling a perfectly good tea bag by not making it right."

No wonder Frank pretends he doesn't hear her. I'm starting to think that maybe he does it on purpose so he doesn't have to listen to all the dos and don'ts.

"Ah, now that's a good cup of tea." She closes her eyes in between sips. Every time she takes a drink, she opens them and glances over at the bag of frozen sheets.

"I guess I can try ironing them if you want," I say after about the fifth time she's glanced at them. I can't believe I just said that.

"Well, aren't you an angel. I was just thinking about them. The iron is in the room by the porch. You can set it up in front of the TV if you'd like." She places her teacup down. It clinks and wobbles before resting still. I notice her hands are shaking.

"Are you sure you're all right?"

"I'll be fine, dear. I'm just going to go at a snail's pace." She stands up but almost falls back. "On second thought, maybe a hand going up the stairs would be a good idea."

Frank is snoring away in the dining room. "Do you hear that awful noise?" she says, clutching my arm. "Sixty years I've put up with that!"

CHAPTER EIGHT

"What's the time, Coxswain?"

"One minute before twenty hundred, Captain." Ruby answers.

"Right then." Frank reaches into the front pocket of his blazer and holds the whistle out for Ruby. His medals clink together and flicker when sunlight catches them.

"Face aft. Prepare for colours at sunset." He then adjusts his sailor's cap before raising his hand to salute the flag.

"The flag," Ruby whispers. "Get ready to take it down."

"Oh, right!" I untie the knot and hold on to the rope. At exactly eight o'clock, Ruby blows one long, loud blast. A piercing sound that eventually floats away with the breeze as I lower the flag.

"What's the sky saying?" Frank asks.

Ruby and I both look at the same time. "It's really beautiful, Captain," Ruby says. "The sun is going down and the sky is filled with all sorts of mixed-up colours, making the clouds go from pink to red to a really pretty purple colour."

Frank takes a deep breath and lets out a long sigh.

I feel bad he can't see the sunset. It is pretty cool.

Ruby and I climb the ladder to the roof afterwards.

"I wonder why Frank does all this crazy sailing stuff," I say while checking things out through the telescope.

"You really don't know anything about them, do you?" Ruby says, plunking down on the floor of the deck. "I thought you were exaggerating when you said your dad never told you about Pearl and Frank. It's kind of weird, isn't it?"

"Duh. Of course it's weird, but my dad didn't make me feel like I was missing out on anything. As far as I knew he was an orphan. You can't miss what you don't know."

I'm starting to sound like Maggie.

"I guess. Doesn't it make you wonder? I mean, Frank and Pearl are a bit different, but they're not evil."

"Can we not talk about it?"

The truth is, I have been wondering about it—and it's starting to bug me. Why didn't he tell me? Why did he lie?

"I'd want to know," Ruby mumbles. "But suit yourself."

⁓

"Who goes there?" Frank's deep voice bellows from his bedroom.

"It's me, Jacob," I say, as usual, standing outside his bedroom door.

"Who?"

"Your grandson. It's me, Jacob." I poke my head in the doorway. "I'm going to bed. Um…I thought I'd say good night."

I'm still not used to the fact that Frank can't remember some things—obvious things, like *me*, for example—but then other things, like how fast a ship goes, he remembers right down to the second. Maybe he's just messing with my head.

Frank is on his hands and knees, going through a plastic box.

"What are you looking for?"

"I'm trying to find my reading tapes."

"What do they look like?" I ask, kneeling down beside him.

"They look like tapes, boy." His voice is full of grit.

I glance in the box he's rummaging through. It's full of keys and padlocks. "Um…I don't think this has tapes in it." I cross my fingers he's not going to get mad.

"If everything weren't in a such a mess, I could find them!" Frank sits down on the floor like a little kid. I study his face closely. His forehead is wrinkled and he looks really sad. "I get so damn-fangled mad I can't read anymore!" He pauses. "Can you read, boy?"

Oh, God. Don't make me read. I'm no good at it. Miss Ward always embarrasses me at school. *Jacob—you can't mumble your way through your readings. Pronounce each syllable.* And then she makes me read longer and everyone laughs.

"Um…I'm not really the greatest reader."

"I'll be the judge of that."

"I don't mind looking with you—it's gotta be here, like you said." I jump to my feet. "What was the name of the tape you were looking for?"

"*We Didn't Mean to Go to Sea*," Frank says.

Of course it's about the sea. I start looking for reading tapes.

Frank gets up from the floor and finds his way to a big chair in the corner of his room.

He plunks himself down with a big thud. "Any luck, boy?"

"I don't see any tapes, just books." A million, to be exact.

"Well, grab the first one you put your hands on then and read me the title."

Seriously? Oh, man. I grab the closest one. "*Canadian Politics.*"

"Next!"

I pull a few more out without reading the titles out loud. I can tell they'll be no good. I shove them back in before Frank asks for them.

"Well? Don't tell me you can't read titles."

I grab another one before he totally loses it. The front cover has fallen off, but I see the title in small print: *We Didn't Mean to Go to Sea*. How freaky is that?

"I think I found it!"

"Atta boy!"

A map of the North Sea fills the inside cover. I don't even know where the North Sea is until I see France, Belgium, and Holland. I start flipping through the pages until I get to the first chapter: "A Bowline Knot." Sounds...totally boring.

"Let's hear some words coming from that mouth of yours. I don't have all night."

All of a sudden my throat feels really dry, like I haven't had water for days.

"Well, let's not waste a minute, then." Frank gets a peaceful look on his face as he waits for me to begin.

I sit down at his desk and clear my throat. "John was at the oars," I say quietly. "Roger was in the bows; Susan..."

"Speak up, boy. I can barely hear you."

"Susan," I say a little louder, and then I stop and stare at the next words. There must be a mistake.

"And..." Frank says.

"Um...I think there might be a mistake in the book."

"Well, what's the word? Spell it out, for Pete's sake."

He can't be serious. "Um..."

"What? You can't spell?"

I clear my throat. "T-I-T-T-Y."

"That's no mistake. Titty is her name. Carry on."

I feel my face getting hot. Who names a girl *that?* What kind of book is this, anyways?

"Haven't you read any of Arthur Ransome's stories in school?" Frank's face is wrinkled up like I've committed a serious crime.

"Who?"

"That settles it. You've got a book to get through. No grandson of mine—" He pauses. "You did say you were my grandson, right?"

"Yup."

"Well, no grandson of mine is going to say he's never read *We Didn't Mean to Go to Sea.*" Frank clears his throat and then says, "Now, I won't have you stopping and starting every other sentence like you've run into a boulder. Just plough through the words even if you don't recognize them."

So that night, I, Jacob Mosher, start reading a sailing adventure about a girl named Titty.

CHAPTER NINE

THE NEXT DAY, AFTER PEARL and Frank conk out for their morning nap, I slip outside, making sure I don't slam the screen door. The last thing I need is for one of them to wake up raring to do something with me. Besides, me and Ruby made plans to hang out this morning.

A tractor barrels out of the lane as I step onto the veranda. "Oh man, that's gross!" I lift up my shirt to cover my nose as cow crap plops off the wagon and splats all over the road.

Nasty. Even after eating Maggie's baked beans my farts don't smell that bad.

I head down the road towards the water. Sure enough, Ruby is on the wharf waiting for me. I plunk down on the bench beside her. The tide is up and the water is as still as glass.

"Took you long enough," she says.

"Tell me about it. I was reading to Frank—had to wait until he conked out."

"I figured it wouldn't take him long to get you reading to him. I've been doing that for a while. Which book did he pick?"

"Um…I forget the name…something about going to sea."

"Oh, I know that one! It's a good book. Titty's my favourite." She says the name like there's nothing wrong with it.

I start to laugh because I don't know what to say. It's kind of strange to be talking with a girl about another girl whose name happens to be a body part.

"What's so funny?" she asks.

"Her name…it's a bit weird, don't you think?"

"Oh, *that*. I think it's short for Tabitha. I thought it was funny too when I first read it. Can you imagine someone calling a girl that now?"

"No, I can't." I put my feet on the railing and let the sun beat down on my face.

"I'm starving," Ruby announces. "Want to get a cinnamon bun at the museum?"

"Yeah, sure."

We walk across the ball field towards the boat shed. Ruby goes on and on about her older sister, Margaret, who's driving her nuts. I haven't met Margaret yet. I wonder if she was the girl on the roof.

The door jingles as we enter the gift shop. An older man is talking on the phone. He glances up, and then quickly goes back to his conversation.

"I see. Well, that's very discouraging news. It doesn't leave us with many options. Are you sure there's nothing we can do?"

"That's my grandfather," Ruby whispers.

The smell of freshly baked cinnamon buns wafts through the air. Suddenly I'm starving.

Ruby drags me through the shipbuilding displays in the main room.

"Oops, I forgot to record the time on the tidal bore chart when I was volunteering yesterday."

"What's that?" I ask.

Ruby rushes over to a chalkboard surrounded by fossils and maps of the area. "It's kind of *boring* if you ask me, but people act as if it's a miracle." Ruby starts erasing yesterday's times. "People come from all over to watch this little wave of water that brings the tide in. Personally, I think they'd have way more fun if they just went out mud sliding." Ruby puts her hand to her forehead and pretends she's upset. "'*Oh NO! We've driven all the way from Massachusetts. When will it happen again?*' I don't get it."

I check out the pictures while she's writing on the chalkboard. There's a photograph of a man standing in front of a building with a post office sign on it. He's wearing a white puffy shirt with a black band wrapped around his arm. Next to it is a shoemaker's shop. Paintings of ships being built and old sea captains hang on the walls.

"Have you found The Captain yet?" Ruby asks. "He's sitting on a wagon full of hay."

I scan the pictures. One has a heading that says *Children of Newport Landing*. There's a boy on a wagon that kind of looks like Frank. He's wearing a straw hat and suspenders. It's weird seeing him when he was younger.

At the back of the museum is a tea room with a brick fireplace and lots of windows overlooking the water. Ruby motions for me to be quiet and then jumps into the smallest kitchen ever and says, "BOO!"

A girl screams and a dish crashes to the floor. "Ruby!" the girl yells. "How many times have I told you—"

"I'm sorry," Ruby says, laughing. "You're so easy to scare. Besides, there's no one here except Granddaddy."

The girl storms out of the kitchen. Her big blue eyes lock with mine as she practically rams into me. It's the girl from the roof.

"Oh, sorry," she says. "I didn't see you there."

"That's my sister, Titty," Ruby says, and then doubles over in hysterics.

CHAPTER TEN

"JUST KIDDING—THAT'S MARGARET, MY BIG sister," Ruby says, trying to catch her breath in between fits of laughter. She then shoves a cinnamon bun the size of a Frisbee in my direction and places some money on the counter.

I take a bite.

"They're pretty good, eh?" Ruby asks.

"*Mmm*," I mumble as Margaret comes back with a broom and a dustpan in her hand.

I wipe the crumbs from my mouth with the sleeve of my shirt and immediately look at the floor.

"We better get out of here before she freaks out again," Ruby whispers.

She grabs me by the arm. "Hey, wanna hear a real foghorn?"

Ruby bends down and turns a crank on an old black box. Low, grumbling sounds come out of it. The faster Ruby turns the crank, the louder it gets. It sounds like a cow dying.

"Easy does it, Ruby," her grandfather says. "You're going to make us all deaf."

A couple that just walked into the museum stands in between the doorway of the gift shop and the main display room. They carry on talking with Ruby's grandfather. "I'm afraid you've missed the tidal bore today," I hear him say.

"Oh, that's unfortunate," the woman says. "We'd really love to see it."

"See what I mean?" Ruby whispers.

Her grandfather glances at the chart Ruby updated. "It's all in the timing," he says. "The tidal bore occurs three hours before high water and rises an inch and a half every minute. So you have to catch it at the right moment. Your best bet is to try tomorrow afternoon around two."

The couple thanks Ruby's grandfather and carries on looking at the displays. He then turns towards us.

"Ruby, is everything okay in the tea room?"

"Oh, yeah—um…Margaret dropped a plate."

I avoid looking at him.

"I thought I heard something. So, who's your friend?"

"Oh, this is The Captain's grandson."

"Frank's grandson? Well, I'll be darned." He stretches out his hand and shakes mine really hard. "I'm Malcolm, Ruby's grandfather." He finally lets go. "Are you here for the summer?"

I nod my head.

"Well, isn't that great. Frank used to come in here just about every other week with things for the museum— that is, until good old Pearl put a stop to it." Malcolm sighs. "I can't stand the thought of history being tucked away in boxes."

"Didn't the foghorn come from Frank?" Ruby asks.

"Yes, Pearl seemed all too happy to have him part with that!"

"Maybe you could look for stuff, Jacob?" Ruby suggests.

Malcolm raises his eyebrows at her.

"I'm just saying—"

"That's quite enough, Ruby." Malcolm hands her a box. "Could you take this up to the office?"

Ruby grabs it. I can tell she's ticked, but I don't know why.

The phone rings.

"I hope it's not the ruddy building inspector again," Malcolm sighs.

"I'll get it," Ruby says, running to answer it. I follow her back into the gift shop.

"Avon River Heritage Museum," Ruby says. She smiles at me and points to the phone while she's listening to the person on the other end.

"Me?" I ask, pointing to myself.

"It's okay—he's right here." Ruby passes me the phone. "It's Pearl."

"Hello?"

"Jacob, dear, is that you?"

I can hear the panic in her voice. "Yeah, it's me."

"Oh, bless my soul. I was just about to send a search party out for you."

"But you told me I could go exploring while you slept," I whisper into the phone.

"Well, we're up now. Do hurry home, dear. Frank has been asking after you. Lunch is on."

I roll my eyes at Ruby. "I gotta go."

"I hope you'll come down again," Malcolm says before I leave. "And stay longer next time. If you have any of The Captain's genes, you'll be a natural fit around here." He shuffles some papers around.

Pearl and Frank must have slept for two seconds. Pearl totally overreacted—a search party? Really? I head up the hill, taking my time. I think about the photographs in the museum and try to figure out where the post office and shoemaker's shop would have been. It's kind of hard to imagine this place being anything other than it is right now, a dozen or so houses on a sleepy loop of a road.

Pearl and Frank are waiting for me in the dining room.

"Lunch is at thirteen hundred hours. Got that, boy?"

"Don't mind him," Pearl says, passing me a plate with three slimy little fish lying dead in some goopy sauce. Their faces stare up at me. "Take as much as you want, I have plenty more in the cupboard."

"What's that smell?" Frank growls. He sounds extra cranky.

"Sardines. Honestly, I don't know why you act so surprised. We have them every other day. Go on, Jacob, dig in."

I think I'm going to puke.

CHAPTER ELEVEN

"You should have told Pearl you're allergic to fish," Ruby says, peering through the telescope on the widow's walk a couple of days later.

"I feel like I'm going to gag just thinking about them." Maggie would never make me eat fish heads!

I glance out towards the water. The tide is in. I keep wondering why I haven't heard from Maggie. She promised to write. Bernice called, but it's not the same. She's all serious and businesslike...

"Jacob! Snap out of it! They're walking up the lane!"

I had completely zoned out, forgetting our morning mission: spying on Margaret and her boyfriend.

"They're holding hands! Check it out. Margaret keeps laughing and throwing her head back like she's in a hair commercial. I think he's gonna kiss her. You gotta see this." Ruby moves over so I can see.

Sure enough, they stop at the big apple tree. Her boyfriend leans in and plants one.

"Smooth move," I say. I feel my face getting red when I realize I actually said that out loud.

"Let me see." Ruby leans in to get a good look. "Boy, they're really going at it. If only Dad could see this!"

"Maybe we shouldn't be watching."

"Are you kidding me? I've gotta have something to hold over her head in case I need it sometime. Uh-oh, here they come."

We both slide down onto the deck floor and peer through the railings. Ruby puts her fingers to her mouth as if she's going to whistle, but I put my hand over her mouth before she can. I don't want Margaret thinking I'm a loser.

~

So I've figured out that Frank and Pearl have morning and afternoon naps, which is when I get to escape.

I've also figured out that on the mornings when I awake to The Crab standing at the front door, Frank is guaranteed to be in a rotten mood. On those days I make sure that by the time he heads downstairs, I'm waiting by the front door with the flag all ready to go. That makes him happy. Especially if I add in, "Morning, Captain. I'm ready for morning colours."

Thankfully, Frank has another helper, who he really likes—Kenny. When Kenny's helping out, everything is great.

Today's a Kenny day.

The race is on. I jump out of bed, run down the hall, swing my leg over the banister in the front hall, and slide down the staircase. I stop just before my butt rams into the square part at the bottom. My watch says 7:04:59.

"Yes! I did it!" Today I beat my best time by one second. I unlock the door and, sure enough, Kenny is on the veranda.

"Howdy, mate. How goes the battle?"

"Pretty good." I hold the door open for him. "So, did you notice? I beat my time this morning. I was a whole second faster answering the door than the last time you were here."

"That's the spirit." He rustles the top of my head. "That's how they win the Olympics. How's The Captain this morning?"

"I think he's still sleeping."

The Crab usually grunts past me in the mornings, muttering to herself about how hard her job is. Kenny is totally different. He actually seems to like his job. Maggie would like him.

"Well, I know how to get the old Captain up and at 'em. He and I just need to take an adventure on the high seas."

"You know, the other lady who comes in never goes along with him with that stuff. She actually gets mad at him when he tries. I don't like her."

"Hey, I'm all about the happiness. And at his age, if that's what puts him in his groove, then why not? Well, I better get the ships a-sailing." Kenny heads up the stairs whistling quietly to himself.

I walk back to my room. Pearl is snoring like crazy. I close my bedroom door and flop down on my bed. Kenny's muffled laughter drifts down through the heating vents.

I lie there quietly, thinking about things—like, seeing as how I'm the only one who seems to hear the doorbell in the morning, what did Pearl do before I was here? Then I remember that her help keeps quitting. And what did Frank do all day before I came? He must have been bored out of his tree. I just can't figure out why Dad didn't tell me about them. Not knowing is starting to pick at me like a mosquito bite that doesn't stop itching.

Maggie always says that worrying only causes more worry, but things are different now, because what I know is different. Dad did have parents, and I'm going to find out why he kept them from me. I'm just not sure how.

CHAPTER TWELVE

WHEN I'M NOT READING TO Frank, Pearl gets me playing cards. We go back and forth between Crazy Eights and Go Fish. She says it's good for her brain. The trouble is, we both like to win. I pretend to lose sometimes—it kills me. The game I like the best is 45's, but you need at least three people to play, so we wait for the nights Kenny drops in when he's not working.

"Sorry, Pearl. I hate to do this to you," Kenny says, laying down the ace of hearts.

"Kenny! You little scamp!" Pearl says, watching her jack of spades getting beaten out. "I'll get you next hand."

I stare at my cards, trying to figure out how to outsmart them both.

"Why don't you tell us a story, Pearl, while Jacob plans his next move. I think I stumped him."

"Very funny," I mumble. Personally, I think Kenny is stalling because he knows Pearl is losing.

"Well, I can't tell a story and play cards at the same time!" Pearl says, slapping down her cards. "I'll need a little nibble of something first." She gets up from the table, walks over to the china cabinet, pulls out a tin of ginger cookies, and places them on the table.

"I have to hide these from Frank," Pearl says. "He'd have the lot gone in seconds if he knew where they were." She looks pleased that she has one over on Frank.

"So, you want a story, do you?" Pearl asks.

"Have you told Jacob about Frank's grandfather yet?" Kenny says. "Because that's a doozy of a story—it's right out of a movie."

I feel funny that Kenny knows stuff about my family that I don't. I try not to let it show, but it kind of stings.

"That's him right there," Kenny says, pointing to a painting of a man in a naval uniform hanging over the china cabinet.

I stare at the painting. The man's jacket looks familiar, with all the medals hanging from the pocket. "Is that the same jacket Frank wears?" I ask.

Pearl sighs. "Yes, it is. I've tried to hide that thing so many times, but somehow he manages to sniff it out. I've given up trying."

I lean back in my chair and fold my arms. Can't we just play the card game?

"When Frank's grandfather was a young boy, his mother remarried after she divorced her first husband, which in those days was frowned upon. Not like today, where everyone gets divorced at the drop of a hat..."

"Now, don't keep us hanging, Pearl. The card game is still waiting, unless you want to call it game."

"Kenny, don't be cheeky," Pearl says, lightly slapping his arm. "Now, where was I?" Pause. "Oh yes—his mother married a blacksmith, and according to Frank, he was a wretched man who was horrid to his wife and Frank's grandfather, who at eight years old was responsible for chopping all the wood for the house—with a dull axe, I might add." Pearl shakes her head. "The poor dear slept in the attic on straw with only two blankets, and during the day he had to help the old bugger make shoes. One day, the blacksmith's temper flared up one too many times and he hit Frank's grandfather over the head with a heavy boot. That was it for Frank's grandfather. He couldn't take it any longer, so in the middle of the night he crawled out of his bedroom window and made his way to Halifax on foot."

Despite myself, I'm drawn into the story, and can't help asking, "How old was he?"

"I believe sixteen, dear. I shudder to think of that poor soul walking on the dirt roads for days."

"Can you imagine?" Kenny adds.

I shake my head. "So then what happened?"

"Well, he managed to get a job at the waterfront in Halifax as a blacksmith, but it didn't last very long, because the building burnt down and Frank's grandfather got blamed for it."

"Was it his fault?" I ask.

"Goolies, no," Pearl says, "but he didn't stick around to have his fate sealed. The little scallywag jumped aboard a ship headed for England with a shipload of supplies."

"Wow! Did he get caught? Did he come back?" I ask.

"If you let me carry on, I'll tell you."

"Sorry." I'm now sitting on the edge of my seat. I've completely forgotten what my next move in the card game is going to be. I can't believe I'm actually interested in what she's saying.

"That's all right, dear. Now, where was I? Oh, yes—as the story goes, Frank's grandfather was put to work in the galley as a cook's helper once he was discovered on board."

"Was the captain mad?"

"Apparently not—from what I gather, he took him under his wing. In fact, The Captain was a bit of a scallywag himself—he couldn't actually navigate out of sight of land!"

"How could he be captain of a ship, then? Wouldn't you have to know that?"

"You would think," Kenny says. "But I guess some people have that ability to fly by the seat of their pants, so to speak. Didn't they flag ships down to get their location?"

"Apparently so," Pearl says, "because they finally made it to England, sold their goods, and returned. By then the shipyard ordeal had blown over."

"Then what did he do?" I ask.

Pearl reaches for a cookie. "Well, he took lessons in navigation and worked his way up to captain on a number of ships."

"Wasn't one of their runs to Chile?" Kenny asks.

Pearl shakes her head. "Yes, if you can believe it—they sailed to Chile to pick up bird scrapings off rocks to be used as fertilizer. Oh my goodness, what was it called?" Pause. "Oh, yes!" Pearl says, snapping her fingers. "It was guano."

This is starting to sound like one of Frank's crazy stories—people sailing halfway across the world to get bird poop.

"It's hard to believe, eh, champ?" Kenny says.

I guess my disbelief is showing. "Yeah, kinda."

"Well, for your information," Pearl says, wagging her finger at me, "back then guano was worth a fortune as fertilizer, and furthermore, your great-grandfather went on to partner with a man in England and built a number of ships right here in Newport Landing at the Mosher shipyard. He even built this house.

"He was so successful that one day, when he was in Windsor on his horse and buggy, the bank manager came running out of the bank to tell him that bearer bonds had just arrived and did he want any—and he told him that he wanted eighty-eight thousands' worth, which would have been equivalent to around one million dollars' worth at the time."

"He was loaded," I blurt out.

"If you mean very wealthy, yes. And he earned every penny the hard way, unlike Frank's father, who inherited all Frank's grandfather's money and did diddly-squat except hide money in the safe and in books around the house. Word was he didn't trust the bank."

I glance over at the painting and then back at Pearl, who's picking up the cookie crumbs from the table. "So, did Frank and his dad get along?" I ask.

Pearl makes a "pfft" sound, which causes her teeth to slip down. She quickly sucks them back up and says, "They were like salt and pepper—couldn't have been more different. Frank's dad wanted him to go into banking, but Frank's heart was set on the sea."

I slump back in my chair. Maybe that's why Dad stopped talking to his parents. Maybe Frank wanted him to love the sea too.

Pearl taps the table with her fingers like she's worried about something. "Frank never made it to captain because his eyes starting causing him grief—and then his world turned upside down."

Just as I'm about to ask her about Dad and Frank, I notice her eyes have become sad, and then she sits up and quickly changes the subject. "Kenny, you certainly are a delight to come in on your own time to play with an old bird like me." She pats his hand. "Shall we finish the game?"

And just like that, story time is over.

Later that night, I toss and turn in my bed, thinking about my great-great-grandfather.

Quick snapshots flicker in my brain as I picture everything Pearl told me. Now more than ever I'm determined to find out everything. I can't wait to tell Ruby.

CHAPTER THIRTEEN

"HEY, WHAT'S WRONG?" I ASK Ruby the next day when I notice her sitting at the picnic table down by the museum. She's slumped over the table, watching me walk across the ball field.

"Granddaddy just told me that unless they find some 'serious funding,'" she says, making air quotes with her fingers, "the museum has to close."

"Why, what's wrong?" I ask, sitting down opposite her.

Ruby sighs. "The roof is leaking and it's destroying important stuff, the doors all need to be replaced, the tea room needs renovating, there's hardly anyone who wants to volunteer down here anymore, blah blah blah. You should have heard Granddaddy this morning as he was trying to open the emergency door upstairs. He was swearing up a storm. I think he forgot I was standing right there. The inspector has given him a month to figure something out."

"Oh, man. That's not good."

"We can't tell Frank, though. He'd be really upset if he knew it might close."

"Why?"

"Frank and Granddaddy dreamt up the idea of building the museum. Together they raised money to build it so they could keep the history of Newport Landing alive. I think they even dumped some of their own money into it."

Everyone knows stuff about my family except me.

"So, do you know about my great-great-grandfather, Captain Frank Mosher?"

"Oh, yeah, Granddaddy loves telling that story."

I shake my head and look over at the boat shed and then out to the water.

"Jacob, there's a whole drawer of information on your family upstairs."

Nothing ever gets by Ruby. She must sense that I'm starting to feel left out in the information department.

"Really?"

"Yeah, but it's not like you're going to find hidden treasure or anything in there, it's just a bunch of journals from Captain Frank, ship logs, and pictures of all his trips—stuff like that."

She doesn't get it. I'm not looking for treasure—I want information. Sighing, I say, "I just wish I knew why my dad never mentioned Pearl and Frank."

"Why don't you ask Pearl?" Ruby suggests.

"I've tried, but she always changes the subject."

"Yeah, she's good at that," Ruby says, standing up. "I was going to help Granddaddy move stuff around because of the leaks. You can help me, and I can show you the file if you want."

"Yeah, sure." Finally I'll get to find something out for myself.

Before we enter the museum, Ruby notices something rolled up in the screen-door handle. It's a local newspaper called *What's Going On?* On the front page is an advertisement for Wharf Days, with a picture of last year's events held down at the museum.

"Hey, you'll be here for it this year," Ruby says with a little excitement in her voice. "Maybe we could sell lemonade or something and give the money to the museum."

"Yeah, okay," I say, shrugging my shoulders.

Malcolm is upstairs moving boxes when we join him. He has the upstairs door open, giving a view of the water. A warm breeze blows through the room. Sweat beads on his forehead. He wipes it off with the sleeve of his shirt.

"Jacob and I can help you," Ruby says, stepping into the room.

Old ship models, paintings, and boxes fill the room.

"You know what, Ruby?" Malcolm says. "I think I'm done for the day." His voice sounds tired. "I'm going to take *Lobelia* out for a sail so I can clear my head."

"Can we come?" Ruby asks.

Malcolm pushes a box to the side with his foot. "I suppose so."

"Are you sure we should go?" I whisper to Ruby. "He sounds like he wants to go by himself—besides, weren't you going to show me some of my family stuff?"

"Nah, he'd tell me if he really didn't want us coming. Besides, we can look at your stuff another day. It's not like it's going anywhere."

I guess she's right. What's another day of not knowing? "I'll go call Pearl."

Ruby and I follow Malcolm down a path through the woods that opens up to a little creek on Malcolm's property, about five minutes away from the museum. After walking through the tall shoreline grass and climbing down a wooden ladder, we get settled on his sailboat. Malcolm and Ruby tell me what to do and what not to do before we start heading out of the creek and into the bay.

Sunlight dances on the water like diamonds bouncing off the waves. I soak in the smell of sea air and the openness of being on the water. As we sail around the bend in the river, the museum appears off in the distance. It looks like someone is fishing off the wharf.

"Do you want to have a go at sailing her?" Malcolm asks.

"Really?"

"Sure, it's a calm day. I'll change position so you can sit here."

Malcolm stands up while still holding onto a long piece of wood and lets me slip in. "Now, this wooden bar is called the tiller," he says. "It's going to steer the sailboat.

There's a blade in the water attached to the tiller called the rudder, and it will make the boat go starboard or port."

"What's starboard or port mean?" I ask.

"Right or left," Ruby shouts as she lifts her head. She's been dangling her fingers in the water.

"Ruby's right," Malcolm says. "Starboard means to turn the sailboat right and port is to turn left. The best way to steer is to look straight ahead at the bow of the boat to see what direction it's heading in. If it starts to veer right then you need to push the tiller ever so slightly to the right and the sailboat will start to turn in the opposite direction, and vice versa. Give it a go. It's a good time to get a feel of it."

I feel an excitement inside that I haven't felt for a long time as I hold the tiller. The sun beats down on my face, so I have to squint as I check out the front of the boat. I move the tiller a little bit to the right to get a sense of what it does to the sailboat. I'm surprised at how easily it turns to the left.

"Now, if we had a bit of wind," Malcolm says, "we'd be going at a good clip. In fact, sometimes the sailboat will tip to one side. If that happens we'll simply adjust our weight to the opposite side."

It feels like I'm now in the book Frank and I have been reading about the kids on their sailing adventures. I never pictured myself sailing before—and yet it feels like it's something I've done all my life.

Maybe it's in my genes.

~

Malcolm is away, and so the week flies by without Ruby and I being able to go through any of the files in the museum. Apparently we'll have to be supervised and wear white gloves to go through them. Ruby says Malcolm is a little overprotective about the letters because of their historical value. So we have to wait, yet again.

Ruby stands up and leans over the railing on the widow's walk and says, "So, you're still good for helping me at Wharf Days tomorrow?"

"Yup."

"Great. I'm going to go home. See you tomorrow."

The next morning, following The Crab's arrival, I hear raised voices coming from Frank's room. I open my bedroom door to listen. Frank's voice gets louder. I decide to slip upstairs.

"I don't have time for your games this morning. I need to get you into the shower. I have three more people to do before noon. Stop being so childish!"

"Don't touch me," Frank bellows.

"Frank—"

"Get out!" he yells.

"Don't you talk to me like that or I'll—"

I open the door. The Crab is red in the face and her eyes look fiery mad. Her hand is raised in the air. She immediately lowers it when she notices me.

"He won't get in the shower!" she snaps.

Frank is standing in the middle of his room with his pyjamas on and his sea captain's hat tilted to the side.

I clear my throat and think fast. "Oh eight hundred, Captain. We need to get you ready for morning colours."

"What's that, boy?"

The Crab sighs. "Oh my God. Not this again."

I glare at her. "Morning colours, Captain. You just need to have a shower first."

"Well, why didn't you say so? Let's go, boy."

The Crab rolls her eyes, waddles into the bathroom, turns the shower on, and says, "Hurry up, Frank!"

"You'll have better luck if you call him Captain," I whisper.

"He shouldn't be living here, you know that, right?"

The Crab's voice sticks in my brain as I walk down towards the museum later that morning. What did she mean Frank shouldn't be living in his own home? Now I know why Pearl doesn't trust her. I don't either—in fact, I don't like her one bit.

By the time I'm halfway down the hill, The Crab's voice has been replaced with the panicked look Frank had in his eyes when she was yelling at him, but as soon as I see and hear all the activity at the ball field, it vanishes.

Ruby has her lemonade stand set up by the boat shed, and there are face-painting booths, games for kids where they can win prizes, a bunch of farmers over by the water getting their animals ready for something, and the smell of hot dogs cooking. The sound of kids screaming and laughing floats through the air.

"Took you long enough," Ruby says.

"The Crab was giving Frank a hard time," I say, sitting down next to her. "I had to stay to help."

"Man, she needs to get another job," Ruby says, stirring the lemonade.

"Tell me about it." I have to change the subject. It doesn't take much for Ruby to latch onto something, and then that's all she wants to talk about. The Crab may have ruined the morning, but she's not going to bust my day. "What's that over there?" I point to the animals that look sort of like cows.

"Oh, that's the oxen pull. They have to pull a zillion tons of metal as far as they can. It's super boring to watch, but the farmers go nuts."

I feel kind of bad for the oxen.

The day zips by, with a game of soccer mid-afternoon followed by the "Hot Dog" event, where dogs race over jumps. The crowd cheers when this little wiener dog finally gets through all the jumps. Ruby and I have the best view from our lemonade stand.

It's really hot, so people keep buying lemonade from us, which is great. By the end of the day it's all gone.

"Fifty, sixty, seventy-five dollars," Ruby announces after counting the money for the third time. "It's not much for the museum," she says, closing the money box.

"If only we could make money magically appear."

And then I remember Pearl's story about Frank's dad hiding money in books around the house.

Maybe there's still some hidden.

I don't say anything to Ruby, partly because I don't want to get her hopes up...but mostly it's because I want to find something myself for once.

CHAPTER FOURTEEN

I CASUALLY OPEN UP BOOKS and flip through the pages looking for money every time I read to Frank now. So far none has turned up, but there's like a million books in the house, so it could take a while. But it's the middle of August and time is running out.

One morning after breakfast, Pearl announces that she's going out for the day. "My cousin Maude has been after me to come visit. There's no telling when I'll be back—she's quite a talker." Pearl fumbles around in her purse for something. "Do you think you'll be all right until I get back? Oh, and remember Kenny is going to be late because he had a scheduling conflict and I told him that Frank would be just fine waiting."

Ruby and I are planning to finally go through the files on my family this morning at the museum, but I can't tell Pearl. She seems pretty excited to get out of the house for the day. She smears on more red lipstick and then puckers her lips together.

"How do I look?"

"Um…pretty good?"

I stand on the front porch and watch her leave with Wendell. I glance over at Ruby's house.

Man, this isn't fair. I don't want to be stuck here all day!

I head to the back sun porch, where Frank is drinking coffee. He's still in his pyjamas. I sit myself down on the nearest chair. "So, I guess it's just us today."

Frank takes a sip. "When is she coming back?"

"Later." My feet find their way to the top of the coffee table as I slouch down in my chair. "She said something about visiting her cousin Maude. She didn't sound like she was in a hurry to get back."

Frank takes another sip. He's quiet for a few minutes, before he asks, "Do you know how to drive, boy?"

"I'm only twelve, remember?"

"What's that got to do with anything? Do you have a brain?"

"Um…yeah?"

"Can you follow instruction?"

"Yeah." I remove my feet from the coffee table. I try to figure out if he's serious or just messing with me.

"Well, then I'd say you're ready for your first lesson."

"I don't know. I mean…what if—"

"What if what?"

Frank is already on his feet, grinning from ear to ear like a little kid. "Are you coming to see a real beauty? Or do I have to do this by myself?"

I jump up knowing I have to follow him. Part of me is kind of excited, and another part of me is worried this isn't such a good idea.

Frank heads towards the back door and down the steps. He weaves in and around the flower beds, knocking a few flowers down with his cane. I walk quickly to keep up with him. When he gets to the lane, he stops every few steps to kick a rock out of his way. It's like he can see.

Sometimes I wonder if he's just fooling us all.

But when he gets to the garage, he traces his fingers around the door until he finds the dusty window and says, "Do you see her, boy?" I feel stupid for wondering.

I stand beside him and peer in. "Yup—there's an old car there." It's hard to make out because it's so dark in there, but it does look kinda cool.

"You'll have to use some muscle, boy. The garage door is a bit stiff." Frank stands out of the way.

I bend down and pull on the handle. It doesn't budge until the third try, when it finally yanks free.

The door wobbles and creaks as I lift it up. I have to stand on the tips of my toes to push it up so it will stay. Once the sunlight floods into the garage my mouth drops wide open. "Whoa! Now that's a car!" I squeal.

"You're damn right. She's a beauty: 1951 Cadillac." Frank goes directly towards the car. A turquoise-green four-door that looks like it belongs in a movie hogs the garage. The dusty chrome bumpers jut out from the back of the car like a torpedo and remind me of a battleship locked and loaded ready to fire. Frank runs his hands over the covered fenders that hide the back tires, then up and over the roof of the car, like he's patting a horse.

His fingers trace down the front passenger's side window until he finds the door. "I don't hear you moving, boy. Are you going to get in or are you going to stand there like a wooden peg?"

"I'm coming."

Sometimes I just like to watch how he does stuff. It's like his fingers are his eyes. I wonder if he misses seeing things for real.

I slip into the front driver's seat and find one big, long seat covered in fabric that stretches over to the passenger's side. A musty, old kind of smell fills my nose. I grab onto the steering wheel, which is the size of a hula hoop. I can't get over how big it is. My fingers grip it tightly as if I'm zooming down a hill, but all we're doing is sitting in the garage. The way the front windshield is slanted makes it look like the window in the cockpit of an airplane. The radio is huge with several big square push buttons to change the station and there's a big round clock over on the passenger's side. I don't see any keys, so I think maybe we're just going to pretend we're driving. Then Frank runs his fingers underneath his seat.

"Aha!" He holds up a set of keys and shakes them. "Pearl thinks she has the only set!"

He smiles and places them on the dash. "We need to run through a few drills first before we take her out for a spin."

CHAPTER FIFTEEN

"WHOA! EASY ON THE GAS!"

I jerk to a stop. The brakes screech like they haven't been used in ages.

The whole gas pedal thing is harder than it looks. We flew backwards out of the garage without me hardly putting any weight on the stupid thing.

"She's light to the touch, boy. For God's sake, don't treat her like a bull in a barn. The old girl drives like you're gliding over waves. Just ease into it and you'll be fine. Now, put the gear into drive and slowly take your foot off the brakes, and *then* try the gas pedal."

"The 'D' is for drive, right?"

"What else would it be?"

You know, I would have been perfectly happy just sitting in the car pretending. I don't like the way he's yelling at me. This wasn't my idea. I press down on the gas pedal. The car sputters and then lurches forward.

Frank slaps the dashboard hard. *WHACK!*

It scares me, so I slam on the brakes, which screech again.

"What are you doing? You're going to make me sick!"

"Sorry. I thought maybe you wanted me to stop."

"If I want you to stop, I'll tell you!" Frank rolls his window down and leans his arm out. He mumbles something under his breath, but I can't make it out.

I take a deep breath and grip the steering wheel tightly with my fingers. I try to make my neck stretch up as far as it will go, but I can barely see out. Frank has no clue how short I am. And then I remember Maggie usually has her seat pushed up close because she's not very tall either. I reach underneath the seat for a lever to push me forward, but there isn't one.

"I can't reach the pedal very well."

Frank rubs his hands together as if he's come up with a great idea, but all he says is, "Minor detail. Stretch that leg of yours. We don't have all day."

He just wants me to drive, no matter what.

I slowly push on the gas pedal. We jolt forward a little bit, but at least Frank doesn't yell or slap his hand on the dash. I go as slowly as possible, but can't seem to avoid the potholes. With each one I drive through, it sounds like the bottom of the car is going to fall off.

KA-CLUNK!

"Oh, Lord, you're going to break an axle!"

KA-CLONK!

"Don't plough through the potholes—go around them!"

I'm so short I can't even see them.

We bounce along the dirt road. His car groans and

moans with each new bump. I expect Frank to say something, but he doesn't. He's hanging out the window like a little kid. I wish I knew what he was thinking right now. He's acting different.

I wonder if he taught Dad how to drive like this.

I get the hang of things once I'm past all the potholes. If only I had a booster seat to sit on, I'd be laughing. The thought of it makes me grin. Dad used to always crack jokes to calm me down when I'd get stressed out.

I stop the car when we meet the field. If I go any further we'll end up heading towards the water.

"Where do you want me to go?"

Frank doesn't say anything for a few moments. I'm starting to think this isn't such a good idea when he says, "There's a road to your left. I want you to take us there."

I drive to the top of the hill and stop. "Okay, I think I see the road you're talking about." But there's a chain across it with a sign that says NO TRESPASSING. I tell Frank.

"What in tarnation? How can I be trespassing on my own land? Get out of the car and see if you can open it. I'm not going to be denied driving on my own dang property."

I take my foot off the brake and the car starts rolling backwards.

"Brakes! Hit the brakes!!"

SCREECH!

"For the love of God, put the car in park before you get out."

"I'm sorry. I'll remember next time."

When I step out of the car, my legs buckle a bit. I take deep breaths as I walk over to the chain.

"What's the verdict, boy? Can we get through?" yells Frank, hanging out the window.

"I think I can get it. Just give me minute." I wrestle with it for a few minutes and manage to get it off the post. On my way back to the car, I glance back at the house. Man, no one is going to believe how far I've driven.

"I got it off," I say, slipping back into the front seat.

"Good job, boy. Now, when you're starting her back up, go easy on the ignition. I don't want to hear a screeching sound."

I manage to turn the key without holding it too long. I can tell Frank is listening to the hum of his engine. This time I don't jolt us forward when I touch the gas pedal.

"So, where does this road go?"

He doesn't answer. Frank is thinking again. We bump along the dirt road. It looks like it has fresh tractor tire marks on it. Man, it stinks. I go really slow because it twists and turns.

The car squeaks with each bump.

"Where did you say this road goes?" I decide to ask again.

He *still* doesn't answer. Something doesn't feel right. Why isn't he talking?

I wonder if I've upset him somehow? The brakes make

a high-pitched shriek like a cat dying as we head down the hill.

Frank still doesn't say anything.

"Where are we?" Frank finally asks when I bring the car to a stop at the bottom of the hill.

I now recognize where we are. "It looks like we've made it to the back of the graveyard."

"How in the heck did we end up at the graveyard? You must have taken a wrong turn. This isn't the road I wanted." Frank wrings his hands together and his voice gets gruff.

"I don't know. I just did what you told me to do."

"Well, you did something wrong! I would never go here. Turn us around."

"Here?" My stomach tightens.

"Yes, here! What is it with you?"

Why is he talking like this?!

"Okay, I'll try…"

"You'll do more than try, Mark, you'll do it. And you'll do it right. I've had enough of this nonsense."

Is he losing his mind? Why is he calling me Dad's name?

"I'm—I'm—not—"

"Stop stammering and turn the dang car around!"

"But…I've never turned a car around, Frank. I don't know how to do it."

"*Frank*? I'm your Pa, for God's sake." His forehead has suddenly grown a thousand wrinkles and his face is as red as a lobster.

My hands shake as I shift the gear into reverse. I push down on the gas and the car flies backwards. I've got to get back to Pearl's. I should have never done this.

"WHOA!" Frank yells.

I slam the brakes.

I can't stop my foot from shaking. I put the car into drive and push down on the gas pedal. The wheels spin like crazy. Manure and grass spit out and splat on the back windows.

"Put your foot on the gas!"

"It *is* on the gas!"

The wheels spin, but they don't take us anywhere. They just make a really high-pitched sound, like a bunch of bees swarming. I take my foot off the pedal and look at Frank. Sweat drips from my forehead. My voice cracks.

"I think we're stuck."

CHAPTER SIXTEEN

THE BACK TIRES ARE SUNKEN in a soppy mess of wet grass and cow manure. I feel like I'm standing in the middle of a toilet bowl.

I kick the back tire. Why did he make me drive this stupid car?

"What's all that banging?" Frank yells.

"I'm trying to get us out of here!" I holler back and then mutter under my breath, "What do you *think* I'm doing?"

This is all Maggie's fault. If she hadn't sent me here, none of this would be happening.

Then I remember that Maggie carries around a bag of sand in the winter because she's always getting stuck. If I had something to put underneath the tires, maybe I could get us out of here.

The tall grass and apple trees surrounding me will not be not much help. I glance towards the graveyard. Rocks—the paths are lined with small white rocks. "Yes!"

I walk around to Frank's side of the car. He's talking to himself, something about, "Can't do it…"

I'm scared to interrupt him, but I have to. "Um…I'll be back in a second. I'm going to get something for under the tires." He doesn't say anything. I don't know what's going on with him. He's never acted this weird before.

I'm worried he might get up and leave, so I run. I grab handfuls of rocks and shove them into my pockets, even my socks. I hold out my T-shirt and dump some in there as well. The rocks dig into my ankles on the walk back to the car. It was probably a dumb idea to shove them in there, but I don't have time to make two runs.

I let the rocks fall out of my shirt like the back of a dump truck and remove the rest from my pockets and socks.

"Who's messing around my car?" Frank leans his head out of the window at the sound of the rocks clacking on top of each other.

"It's me, Jacob." I pack the rocks underneath the tires as best I can.

He's quiet again and then I hear him talking to himself. "The boy—the boy…well, hurry up. A man's got things to do, and sitting around isn't one of them."

"I'm hurrying," I mutter. I'm annoyed and relieved all at once. At least he stopped calling me Dad's name. That really freaked me out.

I walk around to the front of the car to check the tires. *Make sure the tires are straight*, I hear Maggie say. That's always my job when we're stuck in the winter.

They're totally turned to the left. All I need to do is straighten them out.

I feel hopeful.

"What's that god-awful smell?" Frank growls as I slip into the front seat.

"Oh, that?" I look at my sneakers. "Um...there's manure out there, I think." I don't want him to know it's in his car. He'd kill me.

"Those blasted farmers coming on my land. Roll your window up, then."

I roll it up. The smell gets stronger.

Frank sniffs the air like a hound. "It's not any better."

I roll the window back down and pray the stench leaves the car.

"So, what's the report? Is it high tide?"

I stare at Frank. His fingers tap his knee.

I decide to just go with it. I'm way more comfortable when he's talking sailing stuff. I straighten out the wheels. "Yeah, I think the tide is just about right."

"Cast off, then."

I ram my foot on the gas pedal. The wheels spin, rocks fly everywhere, and then we lurch forward. Frank has one hand on the dash and the other on the roof as we fly up the hill. I'm going way too fast, but I can't help it.

"Slow down, boy! There's a chop in the water."

"What?"

"Bring us about! Do I have to repeat myself?"

I slow a bit because Frank looks scared, but I have to get us back to Pearl's. At the top of the hill, I look to Frank to say something, but before I can there is a great SCREEECH! along the side of the car. The sound goes right through me as if a zillion people are scraping their fingernails on a chalkboard. I panic and turn the wheel sharply and end up driving smack into the stump of a tree.

Frank's head hits the side of his window and the steering wheel jams into my stomach. I feel like I'm going to throw up. The car hisses, shudders, and then stops.

Frank doesn't move. He's crumpled up next to the window.

I reach over to touch him. My hands shake. "Frank! Are you all right?"

He moans. I pull him away from the window. Blood drips down the side of his face onto the collar of his pyjama top.

"Frank!" I jump out of the car, ignoring the pain in my stomach, and run around to his door. This can't be happening. "Frank, can you hear me?"

He mutters something, but I can't make out what he's saying. It's more of a moan than anything. He slumps over in the seat. I lean in and help him sit back up. Blood smears onto my hand.

I need to stop the bleeding.

I look around the car for something to stop the blood, but the car is spotless. I search my pockets. Nothing.

Frank moans again.

Sweat drips into my eye and burns, so I wipe my face with my shirt. "Yes, my shirt!" I whip it off, bunch it into a ball, and then place it against his head.

"You're going to be all right, Frank." A big lump

lodges in my throat. My hands shake while I put pressure on his head.

Off in the distance, the gypsum train at Hantsport blows its whistle. The sound drifted clear across the water. This gives me an idea. I manoeuvre myself so that I can keep pressure on Frank's head, and reach my other hand over to the horn. I press hard on the horn. It makes a farting kind of sound at first: *BBBAAARRRRBBBBBBBBB...*

"Come on! You've got to work!" I pound on it. Finally, it hammers out a loud blare, and I keep sounding it, again and again.

"My head..." Frank moans. "What's that blasted noise?"

I take my hand off the horn. "Don't move."

"I'll move," he says slow and slurred, "if I darn well feel like moving. What in tarnation is going on? You're making a lot of racket!"

"You hit your head," I say.

He reaches his hand to his forehead. Blood smears on his fingers. "What the devil?"

How am I going to tell him his car looks like it's been in an accident?

"JACOB! JACOB!" someone screams.

Ruby pedals towards us on her bike. I've never been happier to see her. She throws her bike down and runs over to us. "Captain! What happened to you?"

"The boy can't sail," Frank growls. "We got ourselves into a bit of mess." He tries to sound all put together, but his words slur a bit.

"I think he might need stitches," I whisper.

"Did you say stitches?" Frank says. "I'm not letting any smartass doctor near me. Do you hear me, boy? I don't trust the whole damn lot of them."

I glance helplessly at Ruby as Frank carries on with his rant. "They said I'd be able to see again. Fat lot that did—just get me home."

"How are we going to get him home?" I ask. "It's too far for him to walk."

"I saw Kenny coming over the hill when I took off on my bike. He can help," Ruby says.

"KENNY! Yes! He was coming to help Frank this morning. I forgot he was going to be late today."

"I'll go get him," Ruby says. She grabs her bike and pedals away.

Kenny's yellow Volkswagen bouncing along the fields towards us brings a mixture of relief and fear. I'm not sure what Kenny is going to say to me.

"It's all my fault," I say as soon as he arrives. "He's really hurt."

"Slow down, champ. Ruby filled me in." He places his hand on my shoulder and squeezes. "Not much fun for your first driving lesson, eh?"

"You can say that again."

Kenny leans in to look at Frank.

"What were you doing down the old cow path?" Ruby whispers when I lean up against the car.

"Don't ask me!" It wasn't even a road? Now I feel really stupid. I don't really know what to say. I put my hands in my pockets and listen to Kenny and Frank.

"So, Captain," Kenny says. "It looks like you were trying to skip out on me."

"Fat chance! The boy and I were just out for some shore leave. We ran into a little weather, that's all."

I can tell Frank feels embarrassed.

"I don't know what all the fuss is about," he grumbles.

"Oh, there's no fuss," Kenny reassures him. "Do you think you can stand up, Captain? I'd like to get you back to the house so we can get you cleaned up, and get a better look at this war wound of yours."

"Of course I can stand up! I'm not an invalid."

Kenny winks at me and whispers, "I want you to hold on to one side of him okay?" He then reaches in and helps Frank out of the car. "Ruby, we're going to need your help as well."

Kenny's voice is strained as he helps Frank up.

I take hold of Frank's left arm. I can feel him shaking. I squeeze his hand and hold on tight. He wobbles a bit at first.

"Take a minute to get your sea legs there, Captain."

"I'm working it, aren't I?"

"That you are," Kenny laughs. "If you need to rest, say the word."

The three of us shuffle along, stuck to Frank like super glue. Kenny's holding most of his weight.

Kenny wipes his forehead with his sleeve. "Jacob, you climb into the back and keep pressure on his cut."

I run around to the driver's side and jump into the back seat. Within moments Kenny drives us back home. Ruby follows on her bike.

Kenny stops in front of the house. "Captain, I think I should zip you into the hospital, just to have someone take a look at you. We'll be in and out in no time."

"I'm not going to any hospital. Help me back into the house," he orders. "You can take à look at me yourself."

Kenny glances at me in the rear-view mirror. I shrug my shoulders. Frank is not going to change his mind.

"Okay, Captain. Let's go inside at least. I'll clean your cut, bandage it, and then we'll go from there."

We take him into the parlour. The weather channel is still on mute.

"Jacob?" Kenny says. "In the trunk of my car there is a blue supply bag. Can you bring it in for me?"

I run down the hallway and fly out the front door. I lift up the back trunk. *Huh?*

I'm staring at the engine. That's weird.

"Wrong end." Ruby says pointing to the front of the car. "Guess you don't have Bugs in Ottawa, eh?"

I slam the trunk down and walk around. "Not old ones," I say.

"I should have warned you about The Captain and his car," she says.

"Yeah, that would have been good."

"At least he took you out onto the fields. It could have been a lot worse. Before he went totally blind, he'd take his car out for a spin. Let's just say, he's been in the ditch a few times."

"Lucky me." I grab Kenny's bag from the car and slam the hood shut.

CHAPTER SEVENTEEN

"ALL THIS YAMMERING FROM THE lot of you is killing me," Frank says. "Could a man have some peace and quiet, for crying out loud?!"

Kenny motions for us to leave the room. Out in the hallway, Ruby looks at her watch.

"Oh, man! I'm really late for the tea room, and Margaret isn't going to be there. I gotta go."

I don't want her to leave, but I can't bring myself to say it.

"Are you going to be okay? You look like you're going to puke."

I'm afraid to answer. I know I'm in a lot of trouble.

Kenny's phone rings again. It's the third time someone has called, but he still doesn't answer.

"I gotta go," I say, and turn towards the parlour.

"Is someone going to answer that damn phone?" Frank snaps.

"I'm on it, Frank," Kenny reassures him, stepping out into the hallway.

"You better go see if you can calm him down," Ruby says. "I'll see you at sunset, okay?"

The screen door slams shut behind her before I have a chance to say anything. I don't have a sweet clue how to calm Frank down. I've never seen him this angry before.

Out of the corner of my eye, I notice the book I've been reading to Frank. I grab it, thinking reading might help. I hear Kenny on the phone as I'm walking.

"Yes, I know. I've been held up at the Mosher's house."

Pause.

"I'm really sorry. Could you call Mr. Banks and the others on my list? Tell them I'm running late. I can't leave yet."

Pause.

"There's nothing I can do about it. When I arrived there was a little situation. I need to stay to make sure Frank settles. I'll be there as soon as I can."

I pretend to not listen.

"Okay, troops," Kenny says, entering the room. "How do we reach Pearl? Do we have a number for her?"

"Why do we have to call Pearl?" Frank growls.

He probably doesn't want to hear what she's going to say any more than I do.

"I think she left the number on the hall table," I say, getting up to look. "So, what do I tell her?" I'm freaking out inside. Will I be arrested for driving a car without a license? And what about Frank? Maybe they'll send me home, but then I won't be able to find out about my family. My mind races back and forth with all kinds of what ifs.

"Why don't I make the call?" Kenny takes the piece of paper out of my hands.

I'm relieved. I mean...what would I say? I hold my breath while he's waiting for her to answer.

"Pearl, it's Kenny. I'm sorry to bother you."

Pause.

"Yes, Jacob is fine." He clears his throat. "It's about Frank."

Pause.

"No, no—nothing like that. He took a bump to the head. He may need stitches, but I can't get him to go to the hospital."

Pause.

"I know...it's hard. Finish up with your tea, then. Dr. Bungy? Is his number handy? Okay, I'll do that."

"How come you didn't tell her about the car?" I ask when he hangs up.

"I'm thinking it's better to get her home in one piece before she knows the big picture. The Captain is going to be fine. I would have told her otherwise. That butterfly bandage will hold things together until we get him stitched up."

Kenny flips through a little address book on the table. "Here's Dr. Bungy's number."

He punches in the number and walks away to talk. I go back into the parlour and sit down next to Frank. I pick up the book and fiddle with the pages.

As soon as Kenny walks back in, his phone goes off.

"Not that dang phone again!" Frank bellows.

"Sorry, Frank," Kenny says. Before he answers it, he motions for me to join him in the hallway. "I've got to get going. Dr. Bungy will be here in ten minutes. Do you think you can hold down the fort until he gets here? I'll call Pearl later to fill her in."

"Yeah, I think so."

Kenny writes something down on a piece of paper and hands it to me. "Here's my cell number, in case you run into any trouble.

Kenny's phone rings again. Whoever is trying to reach him is not giving up. Before he answers, he says, "You're a good kid, Jacob—remember that." He pats me on the back and leaves.

"Answer the phone!" Frank growls.

I sink back down into the chair. "Um...Frank..."

"What?"

"Um...I can read to you if you'd like." I look at him to see what he thinks.

"I suppose a man would like that," he finally says.

Some of his wrinkles melt away from his forehead with the mention of reading. Up to this point I'd never realized that being read to could affect you like that.

"Do you remember where we left off?" I ask.

"Can't say I do," he answers, after taking time to think.

"Well, I think it was as they left for their overnight sailing trip."

As I read, I imagine the water lapping alongside the

sailboat like it did when Ruby and I sailed with Malcolm. I can hear the excitement in the kids' voices as they discover all the gadgets on the boat: the foghorn, the ship's whistle, and the compass hanging behind the glass porthole.

I start to feel like I'm *actually* on the boat with them instead of with Frank. I can picture myself pulling in the sails for a full roundabout and the harshness of the rope rubbing against the palms of my hands. I imagine the heat of the sun on my face as I sit holding the tiller. I even taste the hard-boiled eggs that Titty hands out. The best part is that I'm not busting a gut at her name anymore. It's starting to sound like a normal name, not a body part.

Suddenly the doorbell rings, bringing me back to the parlour with Frank.

"That must be Dr. Bungy," I say, putting down the book.

Frank doesn't say anything. I think he's asleep.

A short, grey-haired man carrying a doctor's bag peers through the screen door. He's like the same age as Pearl. I didn't know doctors could still do doctor stuff when they were that old.

He lifts up his glasses up and stares at me. "You're the spitting image of your father. You must be Jacob," he says, stretching out his hand.

"You knew him?"

"That I did. He was a good lad. I'm sorry to hear about his passing. It's good you're here. Now, where is that crusty old coot? I gather he's been up to no good."

Sounds like he knows Frank well.

Dr. Bungy clears his throat before entering the parlour.

"So, Frank. You've been up to your old shenanigans," Dr. Bungy says, placing his doctor's bag on the sofa next to Frank's chair.

"Wha'? Who's that?" Frank jolts out of his sleep.

"It's Bob Bungy," the doctor says loudly. "I've come to check out your head."

"My head? There's nothing wrong with my head!" Frank sits up straighter in his chair.

"Well, it's a good thing you went to medical school."

"I didn't go to medical school, you daft fool."

"Well, I did. So let me have a gander at you."

The two of them banter back and forth like a couple of kids while Dr. Bungy checks Frank's pulse and listens to his heart. Finally, forty minutes later, Frank warms up to the idea that he's going to need stitches.

"So, Frank, I can stitch you here or I can take you to the hospital. What would you prefer?"

"I'm not setting foot in that hospital."

"Somehow I figured that would be your reaction. Good thing I came prepared. I have a local anaesthetic, but you do realize you might feel the stitches?"

Frank sits still for a minute and then finally says, "Do what you've got to do."

"You're a tough old bugger, aren't you?" Dr. Bungy says, shaking his head. "I'm going to wash my hands. I'll be right back."

When Maggie said I'd be spending the summer here, never in a million years did I picture myself standing next to Frank while a doctor stitched up his head with a needle and thread, like a sailor sewing a sail.

CHAPTER EIGHTEEN

I KNOW ONE THING FOR sure: I'm not cut out to be a doctor. My stomach still feels gross at the thought of the doctor yanking the needle through Frank's flesh yesterday like he was putting bait on a fish hook.

"He's a hard fella to say no to, isn't he?" Wendell says, pulling up a chair and straddling it backwards. The cigar he's been chewing all morning is now practically gone.

"Yeah, you could say that again."

"Drink up. Pearl has given me strict orders to sit with you while she and the Doc have a yarn about a few things." He pushes the glass towards me. "It's ginger ale. Don't worry, it's not flat. I opened a fresh bottle."

"What do we do about the car?" I finally have enough courage to ask.

"I reckon I can hook it up to the truck and haul it out of there. Now, don't go beating yourself up. This ain't the first time Frank's bashed the car. Luckily there's this fella down the road who's really good with body work. We'll take it down there and it will be as good as new."

"Wendell?" Pearl calls from the parlour.

"I'll be right there." Wendell ducks out and returns a few minutes later.

"Pearl wants me to fetch some cinnamon buns from the museum. You're to stay put. If you feel up to it when I get back, we'll go have a look at the car."

"I'll be here." I take another sip of pop. Pearl's voice gets louder. I sneak to the edge of the kitchen door and lean into the hallway.

"What do you mean, Kenny wanted me home in one piece before he told me?"

"Now, Pearl…"

"Don't you *now, Pearl* me, Bob!"

Dr. Bungy clears his throat. "Pearl, I think it's time you face the fact that your days of leaving Frank alone are gone."

"He wasn't alone. Jacob was with him," she snaps.

"Yes, and look what happened. He had him out driving the car. Jacob's only twelve years old."

Pearl is silent for a few minutes. I hold my breath and wait for her to speak again. Is she going to send me home on the next flight out of Halifax? Do I really want that to happen?

"Pearl, you need your help back. You can't keep going like this." Dr. Bungy clears his throat again. "With all due respect, I know money isn't an issue."

"Bob Bungy! Just because we once dated doesn't give you the right to tell me what I should and shouldn't do!"

"Pearl." His voice gets deeper. "As Frank's doctor and someone who cares about the both of you, I'm telling you that something serious will happen if you don't heed my advice. We're not spring chickens anymore, in case you hadn't noticed."

"Maybe *I'm* the one who should move into the Windsor Elms," Pearl sobs.

Dr. Bungy softens his voice. "Sometimes we just have to let go, Pearl. God knows I've had to do that over the years. Your house is big enough for you to share without feeling like you're stuck in a chicken coop. We just need to find the right help for you. But Pearl, you have to be willing to accept—"

"Accept what?"

"That if you don't get the proper help here for both you and Frank, he'll end up—" Dr. Bungy is cut short by the phone. I dart back to the kitchen before Pearl notices me spying on her, and take another gulp of my pop.

Then I slump in my chair and hug my stomach. Dr. Bungy is right. Pearl needs help. I glance over at the dishes in the sink still sitting there from last night and this morning. I forgot to do them before Frank and I took our little spin in the car. When I leave at the end of summer, who's going to do them?

Dr. Bungy stayed long enough to get Pearl totally upset. No wonder Kenny wanted to get her home in one piece before he told her about us driving the car.

"Bob Bungy doesn't deserve one ounce of sweetness from me," Pearl says, stomping into the kitchen carrying the cinnamon buns. She unwraps the buns and slaps one down each for Wendell and me. She doesn't even put them on plates. "Eat up while they're fresh."

Wendell removes his cigar from his mouth and places it behind his ear. The three of us eat in silence. The only sound is a fly buzzing around by the window and the odd click from Pearl's teeth.

"I'm really sorry for driving Frank's car," I finally say.

"I know you are, dear. It's not your fault." She pats my hand. "You're a good boy. Your grandfather is another story. *Men!*"

"Pearl, you're outnumbered here. You should watch yourself." Wendell leans back in his chair and chuckles.

"What am I going to do?" Pearl asks in a quiet voice.

"Well, I reckon you're going to have to start looking for some decent help for yourself. Like I've said a hundred times, there's no need for you to be breaking your back when you don't have to."

Pearl sits in her chair and doesn't say anything. She picks at her cinnamon bun, kind of like I do when Maggie gives me lentil casserole for supper. I wish I knew what to say to her. She looks like she's going to cry.

"There's plenty of good folk out there, Pearl, willing to do things your way. You've just got to ease up some."

"Yeah, Pearl…"

"Now you two are ganging up on me." She sweeps the crumbs from the table into her hand, but most fall to the floor. "I thought you said something about looking at the car."

Pearl has this way of stopping and starting conversations on her own terms. She shoos us out of the kitchen, although in a nicer way than she did with Dr. Bungy.

"Where were you two headed, anyways?" Wendell asks, trying to make conversation in the truck as we bounce along the lane.

"I don't know. I was only going where Frank told me. We ended up in the graveyard."

"How'd that go over for The Captain?"

"What do you mean?"

Wendell puts the truck in park and turns it off. "He hasn't set foot in that graveyard for years. In fact, the mere mention of it gets him real cantankerous. You'd think a feller would have made peace with things by now. But I guess death does that to some folk."

He spits out his cigar and grabs an armful of chain from the back of his truck. It clinks as he dumps it onto the ground. After walking around the car, he says, "Well, I reckon this can be fixed in no time. Frank won't even know it had a single ding on it."

Wendell crawls underneath the car until I can only see his feet. The whole time he's under it, I think about what he said in the truck. I wonder if Frank misses my dad.

"Do you know why my dad and Frank didn't get along?" I ask.

Wendell crawls out and brushes the grass off his pants. He leans up against Frank's car and folds his arms across his chest. He gives me a look like I should know something, which clearly I don't. He starts to say something, but then stops himself. "Oh, I've heard this and that…and it's probably more of that than this."

"Huh?"

"You're a good kid, but I don't think I'm the feller to fill you in on all the goings on between your dad and The Captain. I reckon if your dad thought you should know, he'd have told you."

I shove my hands into my pockets and lean up against Wendell's truck. I know he wants to tell me, and it ticks me off that he won't. I'll just have to figure it out for myself.

CHAPTER NINETEEN

THE NEXT DAY, WHILE I'M watching TV, Pearl is on the phone.

"Yes, I'm positive Kenny didn't tell me about my husband's accident," she says. "No, he didn't stay...but he—"

Why all these questions about Kenny?

Pearl hangs up the phone. "Well, that's the darnedest thing," she says, staring at the phone.

"What?" I ask.

"Someone from the agency was asking me a million questions about Kenny."

It doesn't take a rocket scientist to figure out something's going on. One week and still Kenny hasn't called like he said he would. He hasn't been in to play 45's, and The Crab's been coming in even on Kenny's day, putting Frank in a certified cranky mood every time. He's even stopped raising the flag at morning colours, and Pearl is doing more crying than fussing about.

"It's not the same without The Captain," Ruby says as she bends down and ties the knot to the flagpole.

Ruby and I can't break ourselves from the daily routine.

Secretly, we both hope that if we keep it up, Frank will eventually want to do it again.

"He won't leave his room and he doesn't even want me to read to him. I'm just not sure what to do." I sit down onto the grass.

"Why don't you call Kenny? He seems to understand The Captain really well."

I've had Kenny's number in my pocket since he gave it to me, but I've been too scared to call him. I feel something isn't right. It's not like Kenny to not call or show up for a game of 45's. I feel the piece of paper with my fingers.

"Pearl must have his number. Earth to Jacob—are you listening to me?"

"I've got his number," I say, pulling out the paper.

"I've got a cellphone. Call him." Ruby walks over to her bike and digs around in her backpack, then throws it to me. I walk circles around the flagpole until Kenny answers.

"Kenny?"

"Jacob?"

"Why haven't you called?" I don't mean to sound accusatory, it just comes out that way.

"It's a long story. I'm really sorry. I wanted to, but I was told I couldn't."

"Why?"

Kenny doesn't answer right away. "Well, it's like this. The agency I work for feels I've become too close to your family."

"What's that got to do with anything?"

"They said it's clouding my judgment. I should have told them about The Captain getting you to drive his car. He's been removed from my caseload."

This can't be happening.

"But you have to come back, Kenny. Frank's really unhappy and he's giving everyone a hard time. I don't know what to do. You're the only one who understands him."

"My hands are tied. I wish I could tell you something else. Look, I've got to go. I'll ring you back, I promise." He hangs up.

For the second time in less than a week, my legs feel like rubber and almost buckle out from underneath of me.

"I think I got Kenny fired." My words hang in the air as if the fog has rolled in.

"What?" says Ruby.

I tell her how Kenny didn't want the agency to know about Frank's accident. "I guess some of the workers have been looking for excuses to put Frank in a nursing home. Kenny said he can't do anything."

Ruby's eyes flicker. "Maybe Kenny can't, but we can."

The next morning, The Crab pulls up in front of Pearl's house at her regular time.

"What's this nonsense?" she says, in her usual annoying voice.

"Just read the sign, ma'am." Ruby puts it right in front of her face. "It's simple. We're advocating on behalf of

The Captain. He wants Kenny back," Ruby announces with conviction.

On the construction paper in big letters we wrote:

WE WANT KENNY BACK

Kindness
Excellent care
Nurturing (the way The Captain likes it)
Nice
Yoke fellow

"And what the heck is a yoke fellow?" The Crab asks.

"Well," Ruby says, glancing at the palm of her hand, where she has scribbled the definition in black marker, "it means 'a person joined or united with another in a task.' Look it up in the dictionary. Basically, it describes Kenny."

"Humph!" The Crab pushes past us. Before she enters the house, she stops and turns. "Why don't you look up the word *boss* in the dictionary. I have a feeling you'll be hearing from mine any day."

CHAPTER TWENTY

"This isn't working," I complain. "It's the fourth day of The Crab marching past us, and still no Kenny."

Ruby lowers her sign.

"What do you think we should do?" I ask.

"I'm not sure." Ruby heads around to the side of the house, where we we've been storing the signs each day.

I lean mine next to hers.

"Let's go walk down to the wharf so we can think," Ruby suggests.

I glance up at Pearl's bedroom window. "I don't think Pearl's up yet."

"Just leave a note on the kitchen table. The Crab's here, anyways. The way The Captain's been acting lately, she can't zoom in and out like she usually does. Besides, we won't go for long."

Ruby makes things sound so easy. I scribble a note to Pearl.

The birds chirp and chatter in the background as Ruby and I head down the hill towards the wharf. We're both deep in thought—it's like the birds are doing the talking for us. When we get to the bottom of the hill, we notice a car parked out in front of the museum. A man is taping a piece of paper onto the gift shop window.

"I wonder what he's doing. Let's go check it out," Ruby says.

By the time we walk across the ball field, the man in the car has driven off in the opposite direction.

Ruby removes the letter from the window. In big, bold print, it says:

> *REGISTERED WATER SUPPLY*
> *NUMBER 1961–0709*
> *FAILED INSPECTION—BUILDING*
> *MUST REMAIN CLOSED UNTIL*
> *FURTHER TESTING.*
> *Enviroplanet Consultants Limited*

"Oh, man!" Ruby says. "The last time the water test was off, it cost a fortune to get it right again." She tapes the sign back to the window. "I don't know where Granddaddy is going to find the money to get everything done around here."

I wish Frank's grandfather were alive. He'd know what to do. The museum has Frank's fingerprints all over it—it's just not fair to see it close.

"Oh, crap," Ruby says. "I just remembered that today a bunch of seniors are coming out for tea. Let's get out of here. I don't want to be around when Granddaddy blows."

I'm not used to hearing Ruby sound so bummed out. Without even thinking, I say, "Do you want to take me mud sliding?" She's been bugging ever since I got here and each time she's asked me I've made up some excuse not to. I'm not sure why, really. It's probably fun. And besides, I only have two weeks left before I go home.

"Are you serious?" she asks, grabbing my arm.

"Just this once," I say, smiling.

Down at the wharf, Ruby says, "Well, this is where city boy meets country blast."

She takes the tall, shoreline grass. "It's really prickly, but if you push the grass down on its side it won't hurt as much."

She's right, it is prickly—and squishy. Oozing up through the grass, I feel the cool mud. The water seeping in begins to make it really slippery. I can't believe I suggested this.

"Whoa!" I yell as I lose my balance.

Ruby laughs.

I grab hold of the tall grass and pull down to steady myself.

"We've timed it perfectly," Ruby says.

The water is rushing quickly from a bunch of different directions on either side of the mud flats in the middle of the river. I don't know how she can tell which way the tide is going.

All of a sudden, hundreds of birds swoop down near us. They fly so close I feel the air stirring with their flight. I duck. "Man! Did you see those birds?"

"I know. They're neat. They never fly alone. When one goes, they all go. They're called plovers, but if Granddaddy was here he'd say 'semi-palmated plovers.' Sometimes they look like a big black cloud there's so many of them."

Sure enough, when one takes off, they all go together. No one gets left behind.

I bet they never get lonely.

I glance towards the water. "It still looks kind of deep, Ruby."

"Trust me, I've done this a zillion times. It'll probably come up to our knees." She steps out from the shore grass. She sinks knee-deep into mud and giggles at the loud slurping sounds her feet make with each step. I laugh.

Ruby turns around to say something to me and loses her balance. She plops butt first into the mud. We both laugh. Before I realize what she's doing, Ruby hurls a handful of mud at me. It splatters all over my chest.

"Hey!"

"Oh, don't be a baby," she says. "It's just a little mud." Then she flops backwards like a little kid. Mud splats all over her as she sinks further in. She's now totally covered in it.

"You're crazy; you know that, right?" I say, laughing. I step out from the shore grass, and my legs sink knee-deep. I feel stuck and I'm not sure I like the feeling of it. The film of water still on the mud makes it really slippery. Now I know why Ruby fell so easily. With each step towards the water, our feet burp and fart at the same time. Ruby and I laugh at each new sound.

"Watch this!" Ruby says as she stands up and runs towards the water. Midway, she flops to her stomach, causing mud to splat everywhere. She slides down the bank as if she's on a Crazy Carpet. "Yahoooooo," she yells, just before splashing into the river.

When she stands up, I'm relieved to see the water is shallow. It only comes up to her knees.

"Come on! Use the track I just made. You'll love it."

"Here goes nothing," I say. I run in slow motion—it's impossible to go fast. It feels like I have weights attached to my feet. I throw myself down on my stomach and land with a big splat. "Whoaaaa!"

Mud splashes up in my face as I slide down the bank, and flows under me like lava. I laugh my head off as I slip over the last lip of the bank and splash into the river. "That was a blast. Let's do it again."

We both scramble up the bank, each making our own squelching noises.

"Just think," Ruby says before she flops down in the mud. "I've read that girls in New York pay a lot of money for a mud bath—and we have it all to ourselves here. And it's free! Hey, we could advertise this and make some money for the museum. We should think about that!"

I smile to myself as she turns and makes a run for her track. I follow right behind her and land in the water with a big splash. The water is really refreshing and feels good, even if it looks like we're floating in chocolate milk. The current pulls hard at my ankles and swirls around. "Boy, that current is strong."

"This is nothing. When the tide comes back in, that's when you have to be really careful. Hey, let's go to the mud flats out in the middle. It's really fun." Ruby gets up and walks through the channel towards the rippled mud in the middle.

I hesitate. "Are you sure it's safe?"

"Here, grab my hand." She snatches it before I have time to even think. The pressure of the tide's current pulls hard at my legs. It's a good thing we're holding hands.

The flats in the middle are hard, rippled sand that look like waves permanently sketched into the river bottom.

"It's pretty crazy to think we're standing on the ocean's floor right now," Ruby says as she starts doing cartwheels and handstands. I don't bother trying. I'd fall flat on my face. Instead I take it all in. I don't think I've ever been in such a wide-open space before. It's pretty cool.

"A long time ago, kids used to play softball out here when the tide was out," Ruby says. "Wouldn't that have been fun?"

"Yeah. That would be awesome." I turn around and look back at the wharf, the museum, and the mud bank we just slid down.

"Isn't this the coolest? The highest tides in the world come along this shore," Ruby says with her arms stretched out. She twirls about on the mud flats like she doesn't have a care in the world, and for a little while I don't let anything worry me either. Not Frank, not the museum, and not even The Crab.

CHAPTER TWENTY-ONE

"RACE YOU!" RUBY SAYS, GRABBING my arm and yanking me forward. We chase each other through little pools of water and end up close to the other side of the river.

"Wanna slide over there?" Ruby points to more mud banks on the Falmouth side.

"Sure."

We hold hands again to keep our balance as we wade through the channel on the other side. It doesn't feel so weird now.

Ruby scrambles up the mud bank and I follow close behind. At the top, I glance back again at the museum and the wharf. They look like a picture from a postcard. I can't believe how far we've come.

"I think this has to be the most fun I've ever had," I say after we've slid down the bank the zillionth time. "But I'm thinking maybe we should head back. I'm getting hungry."

"Yeah, you're probably right," Ruby says, squeezing globs of mud out of her hair.

When we wade back through the channel, the water is at our thighs, and the current feels different. It's churning in circles, as if it's mixed up about which direction it's supposed to be going. A funny feeling lurches in my stomach. "Does the tide feel funny to you?" I ask.

"Yeah—kinda. Let's just hurry in case I got it wrong. Sometimes it looks like it's going out when it's really coming in."

"Seriously?! Are you KIDDING ME?" I yell.

Ruby ignores me, pushing through the channel as fast as she can. When we get to the middle flats, we run. My heart beats triple-time. Every second now feels like an hour. When we finally get to the channel on the wharf side, it is much deeper. It's now past my waist.

"The tide has definitely changed. We've got to hurry," she says.

Ruby and I struggle through the current. The tide pulls and gnaws at our clothes and legs. It's doing everything in its power to pull us down. Ruby holds my hand so tightly I can barely feel my fingers. But I don't care—I'm not letting go.

Someone yells at us from the wharf. A girl is waving her arms and screaming something. It looks like Margaret.

"What? I can't hear you!" Ruby yells back, letting go of my hand.

The current tugs at me, loosening the hold I have with my feet. I dig my toes into the mud. "Ruby! Grab my hand!" I scream.

Just as I'm about to grab her hand, Ruby loses her balance and falls backwards into the water. She tries getting back up, but the current pulls her away from me. "JACOB!" she screams.

Ruby's arms slap against the water as she tries pulling herself upright. She falls back down. Her head goes under. She comes back up again.

Before I have time to think, I find myself swimming towards her. The tide is so strong it's like I have a propeller attached to my legs pushing forward at full speed. "GRAB MY HAND!" I yell again. She stretches out her arm. "Can you stand up?" I ask.

"I'm trying!" Ruby screams. She slaps her arm against the water trying to steady herself, but the current keeps winning. I finally manage to grab her bunched-up shirt, which is floating along with her. I pull her close until I can grab her arm. "Don't let go of me!" I scream.

From somewhere deep inside, I muster strength I didn't realized I had, and I stand up. I pull Ruby against the current. The tide pushes against my stomach, making it really hard to walk.

My heart bangs in my chest and ears. I manage to get us to the mud bank, where Margaret is waiting.

"Here, grab my hand," Margaret says, helping to pull us up the bank before we both flop back into the mud.

"Are you okay?" I manage to ask in between breaths.

"Yeah," Ruby says. Her voice doesn't sound like her at all. Her eyes fill with tears. I pretend not to notice.

"I'm sorry, Jacob…I thought I had the timing right."

"Oh my God! I can't believe you, Ruby!" Margaret

says. She too is on the verge of crying. "You told me you were just going to raise the flag with Jacob. I had no idea you were down here!"

"Sorry," Ruby says.

"Just because Mom and Dad are away doesn't mean you get to do things you KNOW you're not supposed to do on your own!"

She suddenly sounds way older than us.

"I said I'm sorry."

"Thank goodness Pearl called over," Margaret carries on. "At least Jacob had enough sense to leave a note."

"Actually, the note was my idea," Ruby says.

"You guys better get up the hill before Pearl totally loses it. She was going on about something. She wasn't making any sense. You can deal with her—I have to go to the museum."

Margaret storms off, yelling back one last time, "You're lucky Mom and Dad aren't here!"

"Could it hurt her to ask if we're all right?" Ruby says once she's out of earshot.

"I think we scared her."

"I guess..."

The climb up the rest of the mud bank is brutal. It feels like I have a twenty-pound weight attached to my legs. We don't laugh at the burping and farting sounds now.

A thick layer of mud coats us and our clothing. Mud plops onto the road as we walk up the hill. We're both quiet.

Pearl stands in the middle of the road, arms crossed, waiting for us. "Good lord in heaven!" she wails. "You look just like…" Her hand presses against her chest and her eyes fill up with tears. She can't seem to finish her sentence.

"I'm just muddy, Pearl. That's all."

"Sorry, Pearl, it was my fault," Ruby says. "The mud was perfect for sliding. I couldn't let him leave without going at least once."

"Of course you couldn't. It's just…oh goodness—I'm glad Frank can't see you right now. He'd have a heart attack right on the spot."

I wish Maggie were here; she'd laugh at the sight of us. Pearl overreacts about everything. "Sorry, Pearl," I mutter. "We'll go wash off with the hose."

CHAPTER TWENTY-TWO

I USE HALF OF THE bottle of shampoo to get the gobs of mud out of my hair. Brown bubbles and bits swirl around my feet before eventually slipping down the drain. The hot-water pipe groans and squeaks when I finally turn off the shower. It feels good to be clean again.

I stick my head out of the bathroom door, half expecting to see Pearl for a mud inspection. Thankfully, she's not there. I sneak towards the back staircase to avoid running into her.

On the hall table by the banister, I notice a letter addressed to me. I recognize Maggie's writing. She promised she'd write. It's funny how seeing someone's handwriting can make you miss them. I tuck the letter into my back pocket and head to the widow's walk to read it. I figure the more time I give Pearl to calm down, the better.

I flick the light switch on in the secret staircase, but it doesn't work. I go in the dark. My fingers touch the wall and guide me, the way Frank's do for him.

When I get to the landing, I keep my eyes closed. I've now turned it into a game. I'm practically hugging the wall as I creep along, trying to find the door to the roof.

I can't find the door where the ladder is, so I open my eyes. I'm nowhere near the door to the roof. Instead, I'm right outside the locked door—except it's open, and it sounds like Pearl is inside crying.

I peek through the crack in the doorway. Boxes are stacked and children's toys are scattered on the floor. A big desk sits in the corner with piles of paper on it. The room looks like it's used for storage. Pearl leans against the far window.

"Pearl?" I say softly. She doesn't hear me.

I push the door open some more, causing it to creak.

She turns around and looks right through me. My stomach tightens.

She points to the water and takes a deep breath. "They weren't paying attention to the tide. Frank had drilled it into their heads how to watch for it." Her voice starts to quiver. "J. J. got caught in the current." She turns and faces me. "It was a terrible accident. Your father tried to save him, but he couldn't."

Who is she talking about? I stand there nervously, not knowing what to say or do.

Pearl walks over to a box and pulls out a framed picture. "Frank had me take all the pictures we had of the boys and put them out of sight. He didn't want to be reminded." She hugs it to her chest. "Now with his memory going—I'm not sure he even remembers."

She continues to hug the picture frame, not saying anything. And then she just blurts out, "I need some air."

The floorboards creak under my feet as I walk over to the window and yank it open. The smell of the climbing rose bushes below the window drifts in and fills the room. It reminds me of the graveyard, and then my skin starts to prickle as I remember the small gravestone with "J. J." on it.

"Pearl? Um...I'm not sure who J. J. was."

Pearl looks at me with sad eyes. She goes to say something, but instead looks away.

It feels like forever before she says, "No parent should have to go through what Frank and I did. He had his whole life ahead of him." She takes a deep breath. "He was the light of our lives." She then turns and faces me. "J. J. was your dad's brother."

I don't believe her. My heart beats in my chest so hard I lose my breath. My thoughts jump all over the place.

"I have a feeling your dad didn't tell you, did he?"

I shake my head. It's about all I can do.

"Oh, heavens to mercy, what have I done?" Pearl sits down on a chair. "Things got so complicated."

Why didn't Dad tell me? It's bad enough I didn't know about Pearl and Frank, and now I find out he had a brother? I'm not really sure what I'm feeling. I wish Maggie was here. She'd know what to say to me.

"Your dad didn't have it easy," she carries on. "The poor dear had seen enough in his three little years to fill a book. He needed a home, and Frank and I gave it to him."

"You mean, you weren't even his real mum?" I manage to ask.

"In my heart I was," Pearl says. "You don't have to share the same blood to love someone with all your heart."

I get a lump in my throat. Part of me wants to run out of here, but I can't—not now. Something in Pearl's voice tells me she needs me to listen.

"I tried to have a baby, but for some reason I couldn't. So we adopted your dad—and then, wouldn't you know, the following year I was pregnant with J. J." She hugs her stomach and looks around the room before picking up a photo album. She brushes off dust before opening it.

I shift on my feet, waiting for her to say something. Finally, she says, "Do you want to look?"

"I guess…"

We look at different pictures. My dad looks like me.

"Is that J. J.?" I point to a boy who's shorter than my dad. He looks a bit like Frank. They're standing beside bicycles.

"Yes." Pearl's voice softens. "He was a busy little thing—hence his nickname, J. J. It was short for Jumping Jacob. Your dad was crazy about him. They were two peas in a pod." Pearl wipes her eyes again. "Your dad named you after him."

The lump in my throat grows larger.

She flips the page. There's a picture of Frank, J. J., and my dad on a sailboat.

"That looks like fun," I say, pointing to the picture.

Pearl smiles. "They had loads of fun. They'd sail over to Parrsboro and back. Sometimes they'd be gone for a week."

"No wonder Frank loves the book we're reading. Did you go with them?"

"Sometimes, but I think they liked it best when it was just the three of them. It was their little adventure on the high seas."

Pearl closes the photo album and takes a deep breath. "Those were happier days, Jacob." She shakes her head. "Frank was never the same after J. J. died, and I'm afraid your dad blamed himself."

Pearl blows her nose and tucks the Kleenex up her sleeve, and then turns and looks at me. "Your poor dad swallowed up all his hurt. In a way, I think it was easier for him to pretend that part of his life never happened. I tried to help him, but no one could. As soon as he turned sixteen, he up and left." She looks like she's going to cry again, but she doesn't. She places her hands on my shoulders and says, "So, now you know the truth, and there aren't any more secrets."

The front doorbell rings, startling us both.

"Now, who the devil is that? I'm not expecting anyone." She places the picture frame on the desk.

I try to follow her, but my legs won't move. I take a good look around. All I want to do is sit and look at the pictures. I reluctantly pull myself away.

"Who's that?" Pearl whispers as we're walking down the hallway. "I don't recognize them, do you?"

"Nope." But I get a sick feeling in my stomach as I get closer. The Crab is standing next to a tall lady.

"That's the boy," I hear her say.

CHAPTER TWENTY-THREE

"I GOTTA GO," I SAY to Pearl before bolting back towards the kitchen and out the back door. I'm not sticking around to hear what The Crab has to say about me. I'm now regretting those stupid signs Ruby and I held every time she came to work.

I hop on my bike and pedal fast down the lane towards the graveyard. I throw the bike down and run to J. J.'s gravestone—the little one sunken into the ground that Ruby and I thought belonged to a pet. I kneel down next to it and yank out the overgrown grass and wipe the dirt off the stone before tracing my finger on the letters. "Dad didn't mean to let you go," I whisper. "He really didn't..."

Now things start making sense. I think of the sad look Dad would get in his eyes sometimes for no reason. Dad kept this to himself my whole life, and most of his. I wish I could tell him that it wasn't his fault. I saw how easily someone could be swept away on the current; I barely even held on to Ruby. What a horrible secret to keep to himself. I don't know what to do.

Then I hear Maggie's voice in my head: *Life throws us pickles sometimes, Jacob. The trick is turning them into something sweet.*

Her letter!

I rip it open and start reading.

> *Dear Jacob,*
>
> *I hope you're having a great time with Pearl and Frank.*
>
> *You'd laugh if you could see me at this retreat. We're not allowed to talk, and the lady I'm bunking with talks in her sleep all night long—plus she snores!*

Maggie goes on about her retreat, which is kind of boring. My eyes dart down to the bottom of the page.

> *Being on my own like this has given me a lot of time to think about things and my priorities in life are changing. I'm so thankful for this time and that you were able to be with Pearl and Frank. It's almost like we both needed time to reconnect with what matters the most.*
>
> *Now that you've found your grandparents, we have some big decisions to make.*
>
> *I miss you tons.*
>
> *See you soon,*
> *Love Maggie*

I reread the letter. What big decisions do we have to make? Aren't things going to go back to normal? And then a sinking feeling sweeps over me. Maybe she's tired of being my foster mum.

I flop backwards in the grass. Can this day get any worse?

I wish Kenny were here so I could talk to him. I try not to think about the letter. Instead, I play the summer over in my head. I can't believe I've been here almost two months. It seems like a zillion years ago when I first set foot in the graveyard with Ruby and it freaked me out, and here I am lying in the middle of it without even getting grossed out. I think—no, I know—I'm going to miss being here.

The sound of a car rumbling up the road makes me think of driving with Frank, and then I remember Wendell was picking up Frank's car today from the shop.

I scramble to my feet, grab my bike, and head towards Pearl's. Sure enough, Wendell is over at the garage by Frank's car. "She looks pretty good, eh?" he yells over to me.

I circle the Cadillac.

"Cat got your tongue?" Wendell asks. "I figured you'd be happy to see all the scratches gone."

"I know about J. J."

"I figured you would sniff it out one way or another. So, how does that make you feel now that you know?"

I shrug my shoulders. The truth is, it doesn't make me feel very good. "I kind of wish I didn't know. It was easier thinking that my dad didn't get along with Frank."

"You know, you can go digging around on just about anyone and find things you won't like. I may not have much schooling, but I do know this: you can fill your brain with things from the past, but it will only rob you of right now. You may think I'm talking hogwash, but trust me on this one."

"How would you know?"

Wendell spits out a chunk of his cigar. "You got all day?" Wendell rests his arms on the roof of Frank's car. "Jacob, if I told you my story, I'd only fill your head with more cud to chew on. Bad stuff happens, but you can't let it keep you frozen. You've got to do something with it or let it go."

I glance up at the road. The Crab's car is still parked out front. Something overpowers me, and before I know it, I'm marching towards the house.

"You all right, Jacob?" Wendell yells.

I wave my hand. "I've got something to do."

The Crab, the tall lady, and Pearl are drinking tea in the parlour. They stop talking as soon as I enter. I can feel The Crab's eyes digging into me.

"There you are. Are you all right, dear?" Pearl looks relieved to see me.

I shove my hands into my front pockets and shuffle my feet before I say, "I'm fine. I just need to say something." I take a deep breath before the words tumble out of me. "Frank wants Kenny back. He needs people around who actually *like* their job!"

"Well, I never," The Crab says abruptly. "You have some nerve. What right do you have to say who should be looking after Frank?"

"Frank has had enough sadness in his life. He doesn't need more." I turn towards The Crab. "But you probably wouldn't know about that!"

The Crab looks at the tall lady. "Do you see what I mean?"

"I'm not stupid," I bark. "I've heard you yelling at him. You even said he should be living in a nursing home, and you complain every time you come here!"

The tall lady looks at The Crab. "Is this true?"

The Crab's face is beet red. She starts to say something, but I interrupt her. I'm so fired up nothing can stop me. "You say all the time that they don't pay you enough to put up with Frank, and you make him feel stupid! He only gets upset when you're working. That never happens when Kenny is here!"

"Oh for goodness's sake!" The Crab says. "This is ridiculous! I don't know what he's talking about." She looks at Pearl and the tall lady.

"I know you made up stuff about Kenny. I bet it's because I caught you being rough with Frank—and the way you brush his teeth is horrible."

"He hates having his teeth brushed," The Crab snaps.

"That's because you ram the toothbrush into his mouth and make it bleed! And then you tell him not to complain. Pearl's never trusted you and now I know why."

The Crab stands up and says, "I'm not taking this!" She storms past me. "I quit!"

I sit down in the nearest chair, surprised at myself. I've never done anything like this before.

"I'm terribly sorry, Mrs. Mosher. I had no idea. I'll look into this as soon as I get back to my office. In the meantime, I'll be in touch with Kenny and see what we can arrange."

"Thank you, dear," Pearl says. "We're all quite fond of our Kenny."

"No, thank *you*." The tall lady stands up. "These are issues we need to be made aware of." The tall lady looks at me. "Mr. Mosher must be awfully proud to call you his grandson."

If only she knew. I'm about to tell her that even on his good days, I don't think Frank remembers I'm his grandson, but I stop myself. It doesn't really matter anymore. Besides, Pearl blurts out, "You're darn tootin' we are!" She winks at me and then walks the tall lady out while I sit in Frank's chair.

A wave of relief washes over me as I unravel my fists, which I've been clenching the entire time, only to discover Maggie's letter crumpled into a tight ball in my right hand.

CHAPTER TWENTY-FOUR

I KNOCK ON FRANK'S DOOR.

"Who is it? I'm busy," he barks.

"It's me, Jacob."

He doesn't say anything, so I lean against the door and talk through the crack. "I want to finish reading our story, Frank. I need to know how it ends…" I stand still and then whisper, "Grandpa—please." A lump lodges in my throat.

I hear him stirring, so I decide to open the door slowly. He's sitting on his bed with his shoulders slumped forward. I slip in and shut the door.

"Kenny's coming back," I say quietly, then hold my breath.

"What did you say, boy?" He looks directly at me.

"Kenny's coming back."

"Well, it's about bloody time." He pauses. "Did you say something about reading?"

~

Having Kenny around makes things feel right again—well, that is, except for the museum stuff. Ruby and I had a couple more lemonade fundraisers, but the museum needs way more than we can ever make, and I've searched every book in this house and there's no money hidden. I'm starting to wonder if what Pearl told me about Frank's dad hiding money in the house was even true.

Malcolm says it will take a miracle to find the funding they need. I feel bad. I know how much it means to him. I hope Frank doesn't find out.

Frank is back to raising the flag in the morning. Sometimes it's just Ruby and me in the evening because he's too tired. But we're okay with that. Pearl insists that I come up with a special name for her. I think she's trying to reassure me that even though we're not blood, we're still family: "We're like tar, Jacob—once it hardens it's stuck forever."

The problem is, Pearl has a whole bunch of names she doesn't want: Grandma, Granny, Nanny, Nana—she says they make her sound like she's practically a goner. So I'm kind of stumped. Then it hits me. "How does 'Mama Pearl' sound?" I ask her after supper one night.

She stops what she's doing. I can tell she's thinking about the name. When she turns to face me, her eyes well up. "Thank you, dear. I'd like that. It will make me feel as if my boys are still with me."

It takes me a few tries to say "Mama Pearl" without fumbling. Sometimes it sounds weird, but the more I say it, the more I like it.

I'm leaving soon. I try not to think about it, but sometimes it creeps up and sits in my brain for a while.

Pearl—I mean, Mama Pearl—is ignoring the fact that I'm going. She keeps making plans with me. I try telling her I'm not going to be here, but she just changes the subject.

It helps that Frank has me reading another book to him. It takes my mind off Maggie's letter and what she was saying about us having to make big decisions.

"What's the weather saying, boy?" Frank asks one afternoon before we start reading.

"It's overcast with a chance of rain," I say, glancing out his bedroom window. I'm getting better with my answers.

"Is there a chop in the water?"

"Um...maybe a little bit."

"Not accurate enough, boy. Look through the telescope. How will you ever manage out at sea if you can't read the water?" Frank bellows his orders from his bed. He's extra tired today, so he's "staying put," as he told Pearl this morning.

Smiling and shaking my head, I walk over to his telescope. I've never looked through this one—only the one on the roof. I peer through the eyepiece, but it's completely black. I try adjusting the focus, but it doesn't do a thing to change the darkness.

"What's it saying, boy?"

"Just give me a minute, Captain—there's something on the water I need to get a closer look at. I'll give you a report in a minute."

I walk to the front of the telescope and look at it. The glass piece is clouded over. Maybe that's why I can't see through it. I decide to unscrew it; maybe if I clean it that will do the trick. I rub it with my T-shirt and then take a look inside the telescope before putting the glass piece back on.

"That's weird," I mutter.

"What's the holdup?" Frank asks.

"Just a minor problem with the telescope, Captain. I'll have it working any minute."

"A person could fall asleep waiting," he mumbles.

I stick my fingers in the telescope. There's something stuffed in there. I wiggle my fingers and finally pull out a wad of paper held together by an elastic band. Why would someone put paper in here?

Several hundred-dollar bills float to the floor when I take off the elastic band.

I scramble to pick them up—then unfold the big piece of paper that they were rolled up in.

"Oh, my god!" I gasp. I glance over at Frank, who's waiting for his report. He mumbles something that I can't make out. I go to say something to him, but then realize he's dozed off. I slip out of the room and fly down the stairs, all the while feeling like I'm going to explode with excitement.

"Whoa, where you going in such a hurry? Is Frank all right?" Kenny says, coming out of the bathroom.

"Look what I found in Frank's telescope!" My hands shake as I show it to him. "It wasn't working, so I took off the eyepiece—"

"*This* was in the telescope?"

I nod my head.

"Well, I'll be damned," Kenny says.

"Do you think it's real?"

We both examine the paper with its fancy red designs all around the edges, serial numbers in the left-hand corner, and *$100,000* written in the top right-hand corner. Old-fashioned signatures appear at the bottom, like the way doctors sign things.

"Why, that scallywag!" Pearl says when we show it to her. "I have been searching this house top to bottom for this bond. Frank's grandfather gave it to him just before he died—told him to hide it from his father and tuck it away for safekeeping. Frank's plan was to give it to—" A whimper comes out instead of words.

"You all right, Pearl?" Kenny says gently.

Pearl clears her throat. "Things have been so darn emotional around here lately. I feel like a wilted flower." She wipes her eyes and tries again. "Frank was saving it for...the boys."

CHAPTER TWENTY-FIVE

"You do understand how bearer bonds work?" the bank manager says to Pearl.

"Yes, I do."

"So, what you're telling me is that your grandson found this bearer bond in the house?"

"For the hundredth time, that's what I told you. My husband hid it in his telescope for safekeeping."

The bank manager takes off his glasses and scratches his head. "Well, by law, then, your grandson is due the money. Do you understand that?"

"Would you stop talking to me like I'm in grade five?" Pearl says, sitting straight up in the chair. "Of course I know that! What I want from you is to set up an account for him and deposit the blasted money in it, or we'll take it somewhere else."

I bolt upright. I can't believe what I'm hearing.

"It's Jacob, right?" the bank manager says, looking directly at me.

I shift in my seat. "Yeah, that's me."

"Well, young man, thanks to interest, this one hundred thousand-dollar bearer bond is now worth one-and-a-half million dollars."

My eyes bug out of my head. "Holy. I can't—"

"Jacob, dear, the money is yours. It's what Frank and I want, it's what your great-great-grandfather would have wanted, and I know that you'll do right by it. Frank and I have far too much money as it is. We'll get this nice man here to set up a trust fund for when you're older, but we'll also let you have some money right now. I'll not hear another word on the subject."

And in true Pearl fashion, the conversation is non-negotiable.

∼

There's a knock on my door. Kenny peeks in. "Do you want to go through the papers now? Pearl's given me the green light."

"Are you kidding me?" I jump off my bed. Pearl has decided it's time to clear out the locked room. Kenny and I get to decide what should be kept and what should be donated to the museum.

For the first time since arriving in Newport Landing, I was able to tell Ruby something about my family that she knew squat about. I can still hear her yelling and jumping up and down when I told her about the money. A smile spreads across my face when I think about the cheque for two hundred thousand dollars that Pearl and I handed over to Malcolm for the museum. I think I almost gave him a heart attack.

Pearl has put photos of my dad and J. J. back on the

mantel. "What Frank doesn't know won't hurt him," she says.

"Boy, this is quite something, Jacob. Look at all of this." Kenny moves from one box to another. "Now, I bet the museum would like this. Check it out."

He shows me a picture of the Avondale sawmill that used to be down by the wharf. Balanced on the top of the roof are ten big wooden barrels.

"That's a crazy place for barrels. I wonder what they're doing up there."

"I don't know." Kenny turns the picture over. On the back, in someone's handwriting, it says, *107 vessels were built and launched in Newport Landing. Barrels filled with water sit on the roof of the mill in case of a fire. The mill burnt down in 1884.*

"Well, that's a keeper." Kenny places the photo in a pile for the museum. "So...I hear you've convinced Pearl to get one of those sit-down stair elevators. She certainly has a soft spot for you. I've mentioned that very thing to her several times and she wouldn't hear of it. I have to figure out your secret."

I smile. I'm quiet for a few minutes, and then I say, "I'm really glad you're staying here, Kenny." My voice gets a bit clogged up. "My dad would have liked you." I don't look at him. I just say it and then carry on digging through the box.

≈

Today's my birthday. I'm not sure what to expect. This

is my first one without Dad. I wish Maggie was here, although I'm not ready to hear she doesn't want me around anymore.

The birds are doing their normal squawking outside my window. Gone are the days of sleeping in, but I might just miss their noise. I stick my nose out into the hallway, but the only thing going on is a snoring competition between Mama Pearl and Frank.

As I close my door, something on the floor catches my eye. It's a shoebox with a red ribbon tied around it and my name written on an envelope. I bend down and pick up the box before slipping back into my room. I sit on the edge of my bed and open up the letter.

> *Jacob dear,*
> *It's time you had these. Now that we have you, I'm ready to part with them.*
> *While it was too hard for your dad to share you with us in person, you need to know that he shared you with us through letters. In the beginning it was difficult, but we learned to accept that this was the best he could do. He had a lot to handle with what your mother put him through. The poor dear didn't have much left of himself to share with anyone but you. Please don't be mad at him.*

My fingers tremble as I lift the lid. A stack of letters all addressed to Pearl stare back at me. My stomach tightens when I notice Dad's handwriting. I pick up the letters. Pearl has an ancient-looking elastic band holding them together. It breaks when I tug on it. The letters slip out of my hands and fall onto the bed in a heap. I randomly pick one up and open it. A picture of me skating is tucked inside.

> *Dear Mum,*
> *I know it's been a while since I've written to you.*
> *Jacob is growing like a weed.*
>
> *Remember when Dad used to say I was growing like a dirty weed and that you better stop watering me? I don't suppose he ever asks about me.*

I try to read the rest of the letter, but the words get all blurry. Instead, I gather up the letters. Now I understand why Pearl never asked me a bunch of questions about me or Dad: she already knew all the answers.

I carefully tuck the letters back into the box before closing the lid shut. The last thing I do is tie the red ribbon tightly around the box.

CHAPTER TWENTY-SIX

A QUIET HUMMING SOUND COMES out of the stair elevator. "It's really easy to use. Jacob is going to do a test drive for you," says Kenny.

"Look! It's really cool. You can even read while you're on it and everything!" I stop it midway and push the button to go back up to where she's gripping the banister. "Your turn." I help her into the chair. She holds on tightly.

"You can use the seat belt if you want."

"Of course I want the seat belt!"

I help fasten it and then push the button for her. "See you at the bottom."

"Are you sure you're up for the fireworks later on, Pearl?" Kenny asks as he leans over the top banister.

I can tell he's trying to keep her distracted as she heads down the stairs. You'd swear she's on a roller coaster.

"I'm not an invalid, Kenny. I fancy seeing the fireworks just like the rest of you."

The doorbell chimes as she's halfway down.

"I'll get it." I take the stairs two at a time and slip past her. I smell chocolate cake coming from the kitchen when I get to the bottom of the stairs. Ruby is waiting on the other side of the screen door with a present in her hands and a big grin on her face.

"How come you rang the doorbell?" I ask.

But Ruby just steps aside and says, "Ta-da!"

"Maggie?! What are you doing here?!"

"Happy birthday!"

I'm in shock. I'm just staring at her through the screen door. She's tanned from the summer and her hair is really short.

"Do you think maybe I can come in?" she asks, laughing.

"Oh, sorry." I open the door for her.

She cups my face with her hands and kisses me on both cheeks. "I think you've grown a mile since I last saw you."

I fall into her arms. "Maggie, I've got so much to tell you. But I can't go home yet. We've got the fireworks tonight, and then tomorrow I'm helping Ruby down at the museum, and—"

"Slow down, honey. We're not going home right away. I figured we could use a little vacation together. Besides, I've had enough quiet to last a lifetime."

I turn to Mama Pearl, who's still sitting on the stair elevator, buckled up tight. "Look who's here!"

She doesn't look surprised, just happy. "I'm glad you made it safe and sound. My directions didn't send you on a wild goose chase, then? How was your flight, dear?"

"It was just fine, Pearl." Maggie walks over and gives her a big hug.

"You knew she was coming?" I ask.

"Some secrets are okay, Jacob. I figured this one was worth it." She winks at me with a new lightness in her old eyes. "Now, someone help me out of this contraption!"

Without missing a beat, Maggie unbuckles Pearl.

Kenny leans up against the door frame with his arms across his chest. He has a big grin on his face. Before Maggie has a chance to introduce herself, he reaches out his hand to shake hers. "I'm Kenny. I have to tell you, we've become pretty fond of Jacob here." Kenny puts his arm around me. "We might have to have a tug-of-war over him."

"What's all the racket about?" Frank barks as he heads down the stairs.

"Oh, good! You've decided to join us," Pearl says. "Frank, come say hi to Maggie, Jacob's foster mother."

"It's nice to meet you, Frank," Maggie says.

I can tell she's wondering why Frank's wearing a blazer with all his medals on it, but she doesn't say anything. Instead she says, "Oh, it's so good to be here and to finally meet all of you."

"Who did you say you were?" Frank asks.

"I think we better leave all this catching up for afterwards—otherwise we're going to miss the fireworks," Kenny says, helping Mama Pearl with her sweater. "Maggie, would you like to drive with Pearl, Frank, and I? I'm driving Frank's old Cadillac. It might be an easier ride for you than the back of the truck."

"I'd love to. Is that okay with you, Jacob?"

"Yeah, sure."

Everything feels like a movie as we rumble along the lane out towards the dykes. I still can't believe Maggie's here. It's a perfect night. The sky is full of stars.

We park close to the edge of the bank at an opening where there aren't any trees. We can see clear across to Windsor. Below us is Rock Cove. It's high tide, and the moon reflects its light onto the water, making it look like glass.

I get a shiver thinking about Ruby and me getting caught in the tide, and then I think of my dad and J. J. A wave of sadness washes over me. Dad must have been so scared watching his brother float away. Goosebumps prick the back of my neck and then a bang goes off from across the water and fireworks fill the sky.

"Wow! Did you see that one?" Ruby yells.

Again and again, the sky lights up with different colours and shapes.

I don't know where you go when you die, but I'm just going to pretend that my dad and his brother are somewhere having fun like they did when they were little—and that maybe they can see the fireworks from where they are too.

Back at the house, Mama Pearl says, "Let's get the tea on so we can celebrate the birthday."

"Whose birthday?" Frank asks.

"Frank! Please." Pearl shoos me and Maggie into the parlour. I think she's getting frustrated with him. "Don't you have some important chatting to do?"

Pearl looks like she's bursting to say something, but Maggie interrupts her. "I was going to wait until the morning, Pearl, but if you think now is the time we can—"

"Of course it's the time. Besides, Kenny, Ruby, and I have a bit of fussing to do in the kitchen before you-know-what," Pearl says with a bit of urgency in her voice.

And then I remember Maggie's letter. I've been avoiding thinking about it, but it seems like I won't be able to avoid it anymore.

Dread creeps into my body. I sit down next to her. Kenny whistles away in the kitchen while Pearl tells him how she wants things.

Maggie clears her throat. She looks really nervous all of a sudden. "You got my letter, right?"

"Yeah," I say, trying not to sound worried.

"Well, I've been doing a lot of thinking about what would be best for you in the long run. Now that Pearl and Frank would like—"

"You don't want me anymore, do you?" I blurt out my worry in one big bark. Just like Frank.

"Jacob, what are you talking about?"

"In your letter, you said that we had big decisions to make now that I've found Pearl and Frank."

"Oh, sweetheart, what I meant was, you've been in limbo for a whole year since your dad died, and I was thinking it's time you have a more permanent family."

"What? You mean have Pearl and Frank look after me?" I glance towards the hallway and whisper, "Maggie, *I* look after *them!*" My heart thumps in my chest. I have to make her see that they can't be my parents, no matter how much they love me.

Maggie squeezes my hand, which is clenched in a tight ball, and gently says, "What if *I* were part of your family?"

I stare at her in confusion.

"Jacob, I want to be your mother—not just your foster mother."

"Seriously?"

Maggie nods her head. Tears well up in her eyes as she searches my face for a response.

All my worries vanish. I swallow hard. There are no words necessary—she knows my answer, but I tell her anyways. "I'd like that."

Kenny knocks on the side of the door and pokes his head through the doorway. "I don't meant to rush you two, but Frank's getting a little—how shall I put it…"

"Cranky!" Pearl shouts from the kitchen.

"Nothing wrong with her hearing," Kenny whispers.

Maggie and I laugh. She gives me a squeeze and says, "I think it's time for you-know-what." She scoots me out of the parlour and sends me in the direction of the dining room as if she's lived here her whole life.

I join Kenny, Frank, Ruby, Pearl, and Wendell, who are sitting around the big oak table that never gets used, while Maggie helps Pearl in the kitchen.

"So, this is the big one, Jacob. You're now officially a teenager," Kenny says.

Maggie sings the loudest as she comes in with the cake. Everyone joins in except for Frank. He looks like he's far away again. I hope he's remembering something good.

"Better make a dandy of a wish," Wendell says.

I glance at everyone. Ruby rests her elbows on the table with her head in her hands. I bet she's wondering if I can blow all thirteen candles out in one breath. Kenny keeps looking at Maggie when she's not looking. I think she keeps looking at him too. Maybe I'm just imagining things.

"Hurry up, boy, we don't have all night," Frank grumbles.

"Frank, honestly, you don't have a patient bone in your body. Take your time, Jacob, dear," says Pearl.

Wendell winks at me. I look at Maggie, and then I take a deep breath and blow out every last candle.

ACKNOWLEDGEMENTS

DEEP GRATITUDE WILL ALWAYS BEGIN and end with my writing group past and present, but with a special nod to: Lisa Harrington, Jo Ann Yhard, Jennifer Thorne, Joanna Butler, and Graham Bullock. Their insight, encouragement, laughter, and support can't be properly expressed into words.

To Penelope Jackson, my first editor, who gave me the opportunity to dig deeper, allowing for a richer story to unfold. Her kind words and thumbs up were like winning the lottery, not to mention her keen editorial eye, which I'm very grateful for.

To Whitney Moran, my second editor, for her sharp editorial eye, which helped put the finishing touches on the story, for which I'm very grateful.

To everyone who has cheered me along the way, especially Alison Rodriguez, Nancy Allen, and Johanna Everett.

To my children, Emma, Maude, Rose, and Grace—you make me proud to be your mother.

And finally, to my parents, who have been the best cheerleaders a daughter could ever wish for, and to my husband, Ken, who has always believed and encouraged me along the way. *Ich liebe dich.*